台灣原住民的神話與傳說〈②〉阿美族、卑南族、達悟族

Taiwan Indigene : Meaning Through Stories : Amis, Puyuma, Tao

總 策 劃	孫大川	英文翻譯	文魯彬
故事採集	馬躍・基朗	繪　　圖	林順道
	林志興		陳建年
	希南・巴娜妲燕		席・傑勒吉藍

社　　長	洪美華	責任編輯	謝宜芸、何喬
初版協力	曾麗芬、林玉珮、林宜妙	美術設計	蔡靜玫
	劉秀芬、黃信瑜	封面設計	盧穎作
		市場行政	莊佩璇、巫毓麗、黃麗珍、洪美月
出　　版	幸福綠光股份有限公司	總 經 銷	聯合發行股份有限公司
	台北市杭州南路一段 63 號 9 樓之 1		新北市新店區寶橋路
	(02)2392-5338		235 巷 6 弄 6 號 2 樓
	www.thirdnature.com.tw		(02)2917-8022
E - m a i l	reader@thirdnature.com.tw		
印　　製	中原造像股份有限公司		
新　　版	2021 年 10 月		
初版四刷	2024 年 5 月		
郵撥帳號	50130123 幸福綠光股份有限公司		
定　　價	新台幣 550 元 (平裝)		

本書如有缺頁、破損、倒裝，請寄回更換。
ISBN 978-986-06748-6-6

國家圖書館出版品預行編目資料

台灣原住民的神話與傳說（2）：阿美族、
卑南族、達悟族／馬躍・基朗等著 . --
初版 . -- 臺北市：幸福綠光，2021.10
　面；公分
ISBN 978-986-06748-6-6（平裝）

863.859　　　　　　　　110013521

台灣原住民的神話與傳說

Taiwan Indigene : Meaning Through Stories : Amis, Puyuma, Tao

阿美族、卑南族、達悟族

2

故事採集　馬耀‧基朗／林志興／希南‧巴娜姐燕

繪　圖　林順道／陳建年／席‧傑勒吉藍

總策劃　孫大川

英文翻譯　文魯彬

CONTENTS｜目次

2021 推薦語　以神話與傳說承載原住民歷史　12
　　　　　　　　伍麗華、吳密察、胡德夫、陳耀昌、薛化元

總策劃序　　關心原住民議題的重要入門書　14
　　　　　　　An Easy Book to Enter the World of Tribes

彩繪原畫欣賞

第二冊　阿美族、卑南族、達悟族

1. 阿美族 Amis

故事導讀　河海性格強烈的阿美族　18
　　　　　Of the Rivers and of the Sea　19

1. 種田的陀螺　20
　Votong's Fantastic Top　187

2. 海神娶親　28
　Vay-Rovas and the Spirit Sea　192

3. 巨人阿里嘎該　32
　Alikakay the Giant Child Eater　194

4. 女人國歷險記　40
　Maciwciw's Visit to the Land Without Men　198

5. 螃蟹人的秘密　46
　Story of the Crabman　201

6. 部落百寶盒　Treasure Box of the Tribes

・台灣花東的阿美族　50

・與自然共舞的六個部落　51

・阿美族的重要祭典　52

・絢爛的傳統歌舞　54

・勇士的成長之路　55

・檳榔牽起好姻緣　57

・天賜多樣的原味食物　58

2. 卑南族 Puyuma

故事導讀　Puyuma，團結的花環　72

Puyuma: Wreaths of Unity　73

1. 都蘭山下的普悠瑪　74

Stories from the Puyuma of Dulan Mountain　204

2. 神秘的月形石柱　82

The Mysterious Crescent Stones　208

3. 感恩海祭的由來　92

Origins of the Rites of Giving Thanks to the Sea　213

　・由來之一 尋找小米種子　93

Rites of the Sea (1): In Search of the Millet Seed　214

　・由來之二 向大魚報恩　96

Rites of the Sea (2): Giving Thanks to the Great Fish　216

　・由來之三 請山神吃新米　100

Rites of the Sea (3): New Rice to Feed Myaibar the Mountain Spirit　218

4. 部落百寶盒　Treasure Box of the Tribes

　・普悠瑪的主要部落　102

　・「會所制度」知多少？　106

　・年祭巡禮：猴祭　110

　・年祭巡禮：大獵祭　111

　・卑南遺址　113

　・海祭之歌　114

3. 達悟族 Tao

故事導讀　大海的邏輯　128
　　Logic of the Sea　129

1. 竹生人和石生人　130
　　The Bamboo Man and the Stone Man: The Creation Story of the Tao　219

2. 飛魚之神　140
　　mizezyaka libangbang　224

3. 達悟拼板舟　148
　　Origins of the Tao Canoe　229

4. 林投樹下的男孩　154
　　The Child of ango　234

5. 部落百寶盒　Treasure Box of the Tribes
　• 愛好和平的達悟族　162
　• 與自然共舞的特殊生態　163
　• 傳統的半穴屋與新屋禮　164
　• 飛魚季節來臨了　165
　• 達悟拼板舟的製造方式　167
　• 大船下水祭　169

非看不可的原住民資料庫

• 造訪部落	阿美 59	卑南 116	達悟 174
• 族語開口說	阿美 61	卑南 117	達悟 175
• 學習加油站	阿美 63	卑南 119	達悟 177
• 挑戰 Q&A	182		
• E 網情報站	185		
• 製作群亮相：故事採集、繪圖者簡介	238		

族語開口說
Learn the
Languages

造訪部落
Visit the Tribes

＊ 本套書共三冊，一、三冊目錄如後。

第一冊　泰雅族、布農族、鄒族

1. 泰雅族 Atayal

故事導讀　神聖的祖訓　Sacred Ancestral Teachings

1. 巨石傳說　The Legend of the Giant Stone
2. 神奇的呼喚術　The Magical Summons
3. 彩虹橋的審判　The Rainbow's Judgment
4. 部落百寶盒　Treasure Box of the Tribes

- 泰雅族的生命禮俗
- 不可失傳的傳統技藝
- 紋面文化與文飾
- 英雄戰鬥與出草傳說
- 泰雅族的食物
- 泰雅族的祖靈祭

2. 布農族 Bunun

故事導讀　月亮、百步蛇與人的約定　The Moon, the Hundred Pace Snake and Man's Promise

1. 與月亮的約定　Rendezvous with the Moon
2. 布農之女阿朵兒　The Story of Adal
3. 憤怒的百步蛇　The Angry Hundred Pace Snake
4. 獵人的信仰　The Hunter's Faith
5. 部落百寶盒　Treasure Box of the Tribes

- 木刻畫曆
- 祭典豐富的布農族

- 天籟八部合音享譽國際
- 布農族的分布與社會組織
- 布農族的傳統服飾

3. 鄒族 Tsou

故事導讀　人的團結與自然的界限　Bonds Among People; Boundaries of Nature

1. 折箭之約　The Broken Arrow and the Two Tribes of the Tsou
2. 復仇的山豬　Revenge of the Mountain Boar
3. 被遺忘的祭典　The Forgotten Rites
4. 部落百寶盒　Treasure Box of the Tribes

- 鄒族哲人高一生
- 鄒族的社會組織
- 鄒族傳統祭典：小米收穫祭、休史吉與貝神祭
- 鄒族傳統祭典：戰祭
- 美麗的生態保育地：達娜伊谷
- 鄒族的塔山與死亡觀

非看不可的原住民資料庫

- 造訪部落　　　泰雅、布農、鄒
- 族語開口說　　泰雅、布農、鄒
- 學習加油站　　泰雅、布農、鄒
- 挑戰 Q&A
- E 網情報站
- 製作群亮相：故事採集、繪圖者簡介

族語開口說
Learn the Languages

造訪部落
Visit the Tribes

第三冊　魯凱族、排灣族、賽夏族、邵族

1. 魯凱族 Rukai

故事導讀：綿長的情絲　The Long Unbroken Thread of Love

1. 美麗的慕阿凱凱　The Story of Muakaikaiaya

2. 雲豹的頭蝨家族　The Cloud Leopard People

3. 卡巴哩彎　Kabalhivane: Our Eternal Home

4. 多情的巴嫩姑娘　Balen and the Snake

5. 部落百寶盒　Treasure Box of the Tribes

- 穿越洪水開闢新家園

- 階級制度和百合花冠

- 歡樂的擺盪鞦韆

- 傳統石板屋

- 魯凱族的傳統祭典

- 孤巴察峨的傳說

2. 排灣族 Paiwan

故事導讀：檳榔、陶壺與百步蛇　Betel Nuts, Clay Vessels and Vurung

1. 巴里的紅眼睛　Pali's Red Eyes

2. 頭目的故事　The Chief and Other Stories

- 由來之一 大水淹沒陸地　Stories of the mazazangiljan (1):
  The Great Flood

- 由來之二 紅嘴鳥取回火種　Stories of the mazazangiljan (2): The Black
  Bulbul Returns with the Fire

• 由來之三 百步蛇 · 陶壺 · 頭目　Stories of the mazazangiljan (3): vurung, djilung and the mazazangiljan

3. 瘟鞦韆的愛情故事　The Tests of Love

4. 部落百寶盒　Treasure Box of the Tribes

　• 大武山下的排灣族

　• 排灣族團結的基礎

　• 排灣族的宗教觀和五年祭

　• 排灣族的傳統婚禮

　• 排灣族的喪葬習俗

　• 認識排灣三寶和石板屋

3. 賽夏族 Saisiyat

故事導讀：感恩與信靠　Gratitude, Trust, Reliance

1. 白髮老人的預言　The Prophecy of the Great Storm

2. 雷女下凡　biwa Visits the Saisiat

3. 巴斯達隘傳說　pas-taai: Legend of the Little People

4. 部落百寶盒　Treasure Box of the Tribes

　• 子連父名

　• 巴斯達隘祭（上）

　• 巴斯達隘祭（下）

　• 賽夏族傳統服飾穿著圖解

　• 巴斯達隘祭圖解

　• 回娘家

　• 祈天祭

4. 邵族 Thao

故事導讀：大自然是走向祖靈的路　Through Nature is the Way to the Ancestral Spirit

1. 白鹿傳奇　Legend of the White Deer

2. 長尾巴的小矮人　Tales of the Long-tail Elves

3. 日月潭的長髮精怪　The Long Haired Spirit of Sun Moon Lake

4. 黑白孿生子和祖靈籃　The Black and White Twins and the Ancestral Spirited Basket

5. 大茄苳　The Story of the Pariqaz Tree

6. 部落百寶盒　Treasure Box of the Tribes

- 水沙連的邵族部落
- 農漁狩並行的邵族生活
- 敬畏感恩的邵族祭典
- 邵族祭司「先生媽」
- 孿生禁忌與傳統習俗
- 山水中的杵音歌舞

非看不可的原住民資料庫

- 造訪部落　　魯凱、排灣、賽夏、邵
- 族語開口說　魯凱、排灣、賽夏、邵
- 學習加油站　魯凱、排灣、賽夏、邵
- 挑戰 Q&A
- E 網情報站
- 製作群亮相：故事採集、繪圖者簡介

族語開口説
Learn the
Languages

造訪部落
Visit the Tribes

2021 推薦語　以神話與傳說承載原住民歷史 _{（依姓氏筆劃排序）}

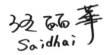

1996年，我回到母校繼續碩士學程。當時寫論文，為了什麼主題煩惱不已。指導教授提醒我，萬丈高樓平地起，既是決定未來往原住民族議題研究發展，應當從原住民族文化的文本分析奠定良基。

這套《台灣原住民的神話與傳說》，對於許多想要認識原住民文化的朋友，或者從事原住民研究的學生，甚至是原住民本身，這是最重要也是最基礎的入門書。

在電子出版蓬勃的時代，特別感佩幸福綠光出版社以精緻的重編再版這套叢書。期盼這樣的心意，啣來更多的新枝，豐富神的花園。

（伍麗華／校長立委）

原住民神話不只是原住民族文學心靈的泉源，也是延伸台灣人民共同想像空間的資源。這本書將原住民神話配以精緻的圖畫，不但可讀性甚高，而且提供很多延伸閱讀的資訊，誠為認識原住民文化的駿良入門書。

（吳密察／台灣史學者‧國立故宮博物院院長）

神話與傳說乃人類歷史之母，口述的神話與傳說是台灣原住民歷史的脈絡，更是台灣史之根源。

身為台灣人不可不溫習自己的神話傳說，熟悉自己的歷史。

（胡德夫／民歌之父‧原權會創會會長）

陳耀昌

《斯卡羅》掀起「探討台灣史」、「了解原住民」的全民運動，讓我們深刻領悟，台灣是「多元族群、同島一命」：

- 原住民了解白浪，白浪卻不夠了解原住民。
- 您知道嗎？台灣原住民是南島語族的祖先，台灣原住民是台灣帶給世界的禮物。
- 了解原住民，請從了解原住民祖先的神話與傳說開始。
- 何況，天啊！《魯凱族》的插畫竟然出自原住民大藝術家：伊誕‧巴瓦瓦隆，太珍貴了。

（陳耀昌／醫師‧名作家）

薛化元

每個民族／族群都有長久流傳的神話與傳說。

神話與傳說雖不是歷史，卻是民族／族群歷史記憶的展現。因此，神話與傳說也成為重要的歷史文化資產。

台灣原住民由於早期沒有文字，神話與傳說更承載了原住民的歷史傳承，而這也是這套書價值之所在。

（薛化元／政治大學台灣史研究所教授）

初版推薦語

總策劃序　關心原住民議題的重要入門書

這一套原為10冊的《台灣原住民的神話與傳說》，集合了原住民的作者與畫者，出版於2002年年底，初版、二版都刷了好幾刷，雖談不上暢銷，但長期以來，它仍然是關心原住民議題的讀者重要的入門書。

2016年，出版社更投入心力，封面、紙張做了更新。在族語語彙的拼法，無法全面改成和現行官方書寫系統一致的情況下，編者們設計了「開口說」的音檔，以掃描 QR Code 的方式（見目錄），直接讓讀者聆聽族語，用聲音拉近彼此的距離。

尤其，2001年之後，原住民各族的正名訴求紛紛獲得官方的認定，目前台灣原住民已經分為16族了，這是我們在人權上很大的進步。這些新認定的族群有噶瑪蘭族（Kebalan，2002）、太魯閣族（Truku，2004）、撒奇萊雅族（Sakizaya，2007）、賽德克族（Seedig，2008）、拉阿魯哇族（Hla'alua，2014）、卡那卡那富族（Kanakanavu，2014）等6族；連同近年來愈來愈受到矚目的平埔族各族正名運動，反映了原住民議題發展的新趨勢。我們真誠的希望親愛的讀者們，能注意這些變化，更深地了解我們原住民的族人。

我們十分珍惜這套《台灣原住民的神話與傳說》系列所積累的將近20年的文化資產記憶，幾經考慮，出版社決定重新編排再版，在不減損其豐富內容的前提下，將原本10冊的規模濃縮成3冊的形式，以降低書籍的成本，嘉惠更多的讀者。我們這次雖然仍沒有能力增補後來正名的6族，但這幾年也看到不少有關他們，包括平埔族，相當豐富的出版物，熱心的讀者應該可以從其他管道掌握與他們相關的資訊，彌補我們的缺憾。

要特別指出的是，這次我們在插畫的處理上做了重大的變革。經幾比對，我們發現插圖用黑白呈現，不但可以避免色彩喧賓奪主的情況，而且反而更能突顯整體畫面細膩的線條與素樸古雅的風格。不過，對彩色有興趣的讀者，仍可用 QR Code找到原畫的初貌。尤其，更值得一提的是，我們這套書的英文譯者文魯彬先生（Robin Winkler），在台灣生活近40年，深入認識了台灣，並更走進了原住民的世界，他以極大的熱情重新潤飾他原來的故事英譯，還增加了「What's more?」和「Where did it come from?」等內容。我們希望有更多外國朋友，透過這套書打開的窗口，認識優美的原住民文化！

An Easy Book to Enter the World of Tribes

The "Taiwan Indigene: Meaning Through Stories," a collection of writings and paintings by Taiwanese indigenous peoples, was first published at the end of 2002. The original and many reprints of the series, while not a "best seller," is established as an excellent introduction for those interested in the indigene of Taiwan. The 2016 edition even included a QR code link for those wishing to hear the vocabulary of the indigenous languages.

Following the series' release in 2002, years of struggle by many of Taiwanese indigenous peoples bore fruit, and the ten tribes recognized when the series was first published, grew to 16 officially recognized tribes. The six new tribes and their year of official recognition are the Kebalan (2002), Truku (2004), Sakizaya (2007), Sediq (2008), Hla'alua (2014) and Kanakanavu (2014). The recognition of these tribes and attention given to the so called "plains tribes" all reflect the development of our nation's "indigene" dialog. We sincerely hope these stories will help our people to follow these trends and gain a deeper understanding of Taiwan's indigenous peoples and culture.

I treasure experiences over the past twenty years and was delighted with the publisher's decision to reissue the books with revised content and format. Without detracting from any of the original stories, the ten volumes have been combined into three so as to make the books accessible to a wider audience. As an aesthetic choice, we also decided to print this reissue with the paintings in black and white – the color paintings are available at our website. While no new stories were prepared for the six newly recognized tribes, we have included much new information about those tribes, as well as information for the as yet unrecognized plains tribes.

It is worth mentioning that the English translator for the series Robin Winker, has since the series' first release, spent considerable time immersed in Taiwan's indigenous culture, and for this series the translations have all been revised and new material has been added, notably the "What's more" sections. Through these stories we look forward to welcoming many more foreign readers to the richness of Taiwan's indigenous culture.

Pae labang danapan

阿美族 Amis

▎小筆記▶

‧運動健將楊傳廣、古金水、陽岱鋼、陳致遠、郭源治；作曲家李泰祥；藝人張震嶽、徐若瑄、范逸臣、A-Lin~都是Amis！

‧天生的捕魚高手，擅長使用野菜於烹飪、釀酒。

・婚後住女方家，把男方衣物放置門外，就是離婚。

・長老會議形成決策，交大頭目執行治理；青年階層組訓為勇士隊，保護族人。

・曾被視為阿美族一支的撒奇萊雅（Sakizaya），2007年經官方承認為台灣第十三族原住民族。

故事導讀　河海性格強烈的阿美族

阿美族是台灣原住民族中人口最多的一族,沿著東海岸和花東縱谷分布繁衍。或許是環境的關係,阿美族是典型的河海民族,擅長捕魚。做為阿美族的男人,撒網的技巧是必備的能力。只要吃過阿美族傳統食物的人,一定會發現海鮮是阿美族最主要的食物來源,魚蝦蟹之外,貝類以及各式各樣的海藻,都是他們的佳餚。海,因而對阿美族來說具有獨特的地位。我們從他們那麼重視海祭,便可見一斑。

螃蟹人長得特別快,他指涉一個具有海洋因子的族類,如何擁有優秀的體格!看來阿美族在各項體育競賽中,之所以能有那麼卓越的表現,並非是偶然的。

從地底冒出來的福杜茲和莎法,應當是大地之神,難怪他們生出來的寶寶福通會製作陀螺(工具的象徵),快速墾植荒地。福通迎娶撒奇萊雅祖先的女兒莎樣為妻,但終因神人兩路而永隔。只是從登天梯上摔下來不幸死亡的莎樣,卻成了鹿、豬、蛇等野生物類的母親,她是大地之母。

福通的妹妹懷露法絲,育有一位全身散發紅光的女兒芝希麗蓢。芝希麗蓢被海神看上了,威脅發洪水強迫屬於大地之神後裔的懷露法絲就範。為了拯救部落,芝希麗蓢終於嫁給海神。傷心的懷露法絲,拄著鐵杖沿著海岸日夜不停地尋找愛女,最後施行法術丟下鐵杖,獨自走回拿拉拉扎南部落。海與陸地的界線就這樣決定了。

阿美族的文化與社會裡,還有兩個突出的特徵,那就是他們嚴密的男子年齡組織,以及發達的母系社會。巨人阿里嘎該的故事,說明了阿美族男子年齡組織的起源,當然是阿美部落防衛力量的表現!而馬糾糾誤闖女人國,歷盡驚嚇之後,脫險返回故里;雖有如南柯一夢,但卻充分地反映了阿美族婦女在阿美族社會裡,不可搖撼的地位和威力。

Reader's Guide　　# Of the Rivers and of the Sea

Amis is the most populous group of indigenous peoples in Taiwan. They thrive along Taiwan's east coast and the rift valley running between Hualien and Taidong. Likely on account of their environment, the Amis are a typical river and sea people, very skilled at fishing. All Amis me are expected to achieve a high level of skill in casting nets. Anyone who has eaten traditional Amis food is bound to discover that seafood is the mainstay. In addition to fish, shrimp and crab, shellfish and all kinds of seaweed are their delicacies. The sea therefore has a unique position for the Amis. This is reflected in the great importance attached to their various rites of the sea.

We see in the story of the Crabman a person maturing exceptionally fast as if a part of the ocean. The outstanding physique and performance of Amis in various competitive sports is no accident.

As *Votoc* and *Savak* emerged from the earth and are considered the creators of the earth, it was no wonder that their child *Votong* would make tops (symbols of tools) and quickly cultivate wasteland. *Votong* married *Sayan*, the recognized ancestor of the *Sakizaya*, but fate would separate them forever. *Sayan* fell off the ladder to the heavens, and while her death was unfortunate, through her death she became the mother of deer, pigs, snakes and other wild animals. She is the mother of the earth.

Votong's younger sister, *Vay Rovas* gave birth to beautiful daughter *Cisiringan* who was taken by the sea god *Kafit* after he threatened to flood the earthly realm. The despondent Vay Rovas, iron rod in hand, set out to find her daughter. For countless days and nights she travelled the coast, finally casting a spell and forsaking the iron rod before returning to her village of *Nararacanan*. The geologic features of the sea and the land were determined by *Vay Rovas* and her iron rod.

Two outstanding features In the culture and society of the Amis are their closely knit male organizations and a developed matrilineal society. The story of the giant *Alikakay* illustrates the origin of the Ami men's organization, and is a great example of the power of the Amis defense forces! On the other hand, *Maciwciw's* entry into the country of women was totally by accident. After he recovers from his shock, makes his escape and returns to his home we see it as a dream. Nevertheless, this story of *Maciwciw's* "Visit to the Land Without Men", although seeming to have been a dream, fully reflects the unshakable status and might of women in Amis society.

種田的陀螺

> 福通把做好的陀螺朝田裡甩過去，沒多久，
> 就把田開墾好了，大家才知道福通具有神奇
> 的力量，對於他所教導有關播種、祭祀以及
> 禁忌的要求，阿美族人謹記在心，一代傳一
> 代。

 What's more?

福通（Votong）：因為會製作陀螺開墾田地（有的故事說他會製作漁具、梯子），所以在阿美族人心目中是個聰明的發明家，族人通常也稱聰明的人為福通或福通之子（Wawa ni Fotong）。

很久以前，有一個男子名字叫福杜茲，和一位名叫做莎法的女子結為夫妻。據說他們兩人都是從拿拉扎南的地底冒出來。不久，福杜茲和莎法生下一個可愛的寶寶，叫做福通。

當時，還有一位名字叫古露米的女子，她和女兒莎樣住在一起。沒有人知道她們從那裡來，後人只知道她們是阿美族撒奇萊雅人的祖先。

有一天早上，莎樣和往常一樣拿著水桶到水井提水。她正要將水提上來時，不知什麼原因，繩子竟然拉不動。莎樣只好回家，並且把這件怪事告訴母親。莎樣的母親要她回去再試試看；當莎樣回去時，從水井中突然爬出了一名男子，他正是福通。

福通一看見莎樣，就喜歡上她，並向莎樣求婚。

莎樣雖然打從心裡也喜歡福通，但是她卻不敢自己做決定，畢竟結婚這件大事應該要經過母親的同意。於是，莎樣帶福通回家，並向母親說明。

母親看了看福通，覺得他長得還不錯，也感受到福通對莎樣的心意，便同意他們結為夫妻。福通和莎樣結婚後，住在古露米的家中。但是福通不喜歡工作，每天只會待在家裡專心製作陀螺。

古露米對於福通的懶散，非常不高興，想盡辦法要把他趕走。可是福通不肯走，古露米找了許多人來抬他，但是不管動用多少人、使出多少力氣，

 What's more?

拿拉扎南（Nararacanan）：位在花蓮港附近，現今港口設施以及房舍林立，無法辨認出任何的遺跡。

阿美族：花蓮地區的阿美族稱自己為邦查（Pangcah），而大部分台東的阿美族則自稱為阿米斯（Amis），這種稱呼上的差別大致以台東縣池上鄉、鹿野鄉為界線。「邦查」似乎有「人」的意思，而「阿米斯」根據學者研究是借用卑南族語「北方人」來做為自稱。究竟事實如何，還需要再做進一步的考證。今日阿美族的族稱則是由阿米斯（Amis）而來的。

就是沒辦法移動他半步。

有一天，福通做好陀螺之後，走到雜草叢生、還未開墾的荒地。他把陀螺用力甩打出去，陀螺一直轉、一直轉，竟然就把荒地開墾成為良田。

接著，福通繼續種下甜的瓜子和苦的瓜子，甜的瓜子生出稻米，而苦的瓜子則生出小米，讓人驚訝不已。

之後，福通又教導眾人播種方法、祭祀儀式和種種禁忌要求。這時候大家才知道原來福通不是普通人，他具有神奇的力量，沒有人再敢干涉他做任何事了。

過了三年，福通向莎樣表示要回自己的父母家，但是路途非常遙遠又很辛苦，因此他希望莎樣能夠留下來，陪在她自己的母親身邊。

然而，已經懷孕的莎樣還是堅持要跟福通一起回家。

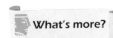

What's more?

撒奇萊雅人（Sakizaya）：這群人主要居住在花蓮市區，因與清朝政府作戰緣故，而遷至花蓮其他地區。他們的語言非常特殊，與阿美族語無法相通，有學者認為他們的語言比阿美族語保存較多的古老詞彙。

一般人多半將阿美族分成南勢、中部、海岸、卑南、恆春等五群，不過在阿美族人認知裡，並沒有任何的區分。

水桶：一般來說早期的阿美族用竹筒舀水，並以一種陶製的容器阿多莫（atoma）來盛水，婦女通常將其頂於頭上搬運。可見阿美族很早就已發展製陶技術，至今仍有部落會製作阿美族傳統陶器，例如馬太鞍等。

水井（tfon，德封）：當初莎樣取水的水井，阿美族人稱為福通池（Tfon-no-Votong）。還有一種說法，認為福通池是福通捕魚的地方，現在已被填平蓋了花蓮機場，只剩下前花蓮師範學院門前的小水池供後人憑弔。

求婚（masunanam，麻蘇拿南）：根據早期的記載，阿美族男女雙方若是有訂婚之意，男方將其頸飾交給女方，女方將其頭巾交給男方，即完成訂婚儀式。若是要解除婚約，則將物品退還即可。

福通的家在天上，必須爬上一座通往天上的梯子。福通和莎樣不知走了多少路，才到達放梯子的地方。

當他們正要踏上梯子時，福通小心謹慎的吩咐莎樣：「爬梯子的時候，千萬不可以發出任何聲響。」莎樣答應了。

他們一步步地往上爬，眼看著只剩下最後一步就可以到達天上，莎樣因為太過疲勞，不自覺地發出「唉！」的嘆氣聲。

梯子立刻扭曲變形，甚至整個從天空掉落到地面，莎樣也摔了下來，當場斷氣死亡。這個時候從莎樣的肚子裡跑出了鹿、豬和蛇等動物，從此以後世上便出現了各種不同的生物。

福通眼看著莎樣摔落地面，營救不及，只能看著悲劇發生。他傷心欲絕，獨自回到天上。而他們所使用的梯子，至今還殘留在花蓮縣瑞穗鄉舞鶴台地上。

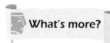

What's more?

結婚（pataloma'，巴達魯瑪）：由於阿美族為母系社會，婚姻關係以女性為主。結婚當天早上，新郎必須親自頂一壺清水到自己家中，表示飲水思源；再扛一擔柴薪到女方家中，代表薪火相傳。結婚儀式則在女方家中進行，女方的雙親會送給新郎兩件物品：一件是開山刀，象徵責任，另一件為情人袋，表示從此是一家人；而新娘會送新郎一顆檳榔代表忠貞的愛情。

陀螺（'acocol，阿祖祖勒）：根據早期的記載，阿美族有關陀螺的遊戲和漢人大同小異，也是以麻繩纏繞甩打出去，陀螺兩兩相碰，最後才倒者為勝利。

祭祀儀式（salisin，沙立信）：根據記載，撒奇萊雅人在早期曾經舉行過播粟祭（mitway，米德外），長達七天之久，後來因為水稻引進才漸漸失傳。

禁忌：以撒奇萊雅人的七天播粟祭禁忌為例，第三天不可以吃蔬菜和白肉（如雞、魚等），第四、五天不可以洗澡、洗手，認為會把土給洗掉，種子就不會發芽。另外，從第一天至第五天，男女之間不可以行房，以免觸犯神明。

Where did it come from?
本故事採集自德興部落（花蓮市國富里）。

 What's more?

懷孕（puyapuy，布雅布伊）：根據記載，孕婦在懷孕時不可以吃雙生檳榔與雙生香蕉，因為阿美認為雙胞胎是不吉祥的徵兆；另外，不可對老人無理，不可說謊，不可大聲罵人，不可淫亂，禁止殺生，禁止接觸死者等。這些禁忌雖然平常族人也要遵守，但對孕婦的要求更為嚴格，觸犯這些禁忌，族人認為會流產。

鹿、豬、蛇：故事中的莎樣肚子裡跑出鹿、豬、蛇等，還有一種說法是出現了蛇、鱷魚、烏龜等，從此以後世上才出現了爬蟲類生物。

舞鶴台地（sapad，掃叭）：故事中福通和莎樣所爬的梯子，正確位置比較接近馬力雲部落（maifor，馬伊富兒），阿美族人習慣稱為掃叭石柱，目前當地有兩根大石柱（原先有三根），是花東縱谷有名的考古遺址。

02

海神娶親

> 海神愛上美麗的芝希麗蘭，祂以淹沒陸地要脅阿美族人，族人只好犧牲芝希麗蘭，嫁給海神為妻。
>
> 忍痛割捨愛女的懷露法絲，帶著鐵手杖，沿著海岸不停的往南走，想要尋回消失在大海中的芝希麗蘭。

原來擁有神奇力量的福通，正是福杜茲和莎法的兒子，他們還有一個女兒，名叫懷露法絲。

懷露法絲生了一個女兒，名叫芝希麗蒳。芝希麗蒳長得非常漂亮，而且全身散發紅色的微光。

有一天，芝希麗蒳到海邊遊玩；海神看見她，萌生愛意，決心要娶她為妻。

海神告訴芝希麗蒳的母親懷露法絲，如果她不答應婚事，就要引海水來淹沒部落。懷露法絲不願接受海神的要脅，打算置之不理。

然而，海水不斷地高漲起來。拿拉拉扎南部落的人紛紛向懷露法絲請求，希望她將芝希麗蒳嫁給海神，拯救部落。懷露法絲雖然捨不得女兒，但是為了部落，迫不得已只好答應。

懷露法絲將芝希麗蒳裝入籃子內，放到海上，任其漂流。不久，海面出現異象，一大片海水突然泛紅；接著，海水漸漸退去，而芝希麗蒳也消失無蹤。

海水退去後，懷露法絲帶著一根鐵棒做為手杖，追隨籃子漂流的方向找尋女兒。她沿著海岸往南走，日夜不停地走，一直走到達拉瓦烙，仍然沒有看到女兒的蹤影。

懷露法絲傷心難過地丟下鐵手杖，獨自走回到拿拉拉扎南部落。

懷露法絲在海岸奔走尋找時，曾面向海水施法術，以鐵手杖為界，命令海水不可侵犯，藉此順利行走，傳說中海水和陸地的界線就這樣決定了。

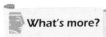
What's more?

海神（Kafit，卡非特）：屬於南勢阿美的海祭祭祀對象。

Where did it come from?
本故事採集自德興部落（花蓮市國富里）。

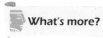

What's more?

達拉瓦烙（Tarawadaw）：相傳位在今秀姑巒溪出海口。

法術（karam，軋蘭姆）：在阿美族社會裡，只有祭司（cikawasa，基軋瓦賽）才有資格與能力施行法術。

巨人阿里嘎該

> 阿里嘎該不只身軀巨大嚇人，還會變法術危害
> 阿美族人。族人組成戰鬥力旺盛的勇士隊，並
> 遵照海神的指示，順利擊退了阿里嘎該。
>
> 為了感念海神相助，阿美族人每年舉辦海祭；
> 並嚴格訓練部落青年的體能與戰技，以便隨時
> 保護家園。

在部落附近的巴力克山上，住著一個巨人。阿美族人稱他為阿里嘎該。巨人阿里嘎該會法術，常常變成一般人的模樣來騷擾阿美族人，甚至造成危害。巨人阿里嘎該尤其喜歡吃小孩子的內臟。

有一天，一位母親帶著兩個女兒到田裡工作。八歲的大女兒已經懂事，而且可以幫忙家務，母親便吩咐她要好好照顧剛出生的小女嬰。於是，大女兒揹著還沒斷奶的小女嬰，跟著媽媽在田裏工作。

到了中午，母親正準備要餵小女嬰吃奶，大女兒感到很奇怪，便問母親說：「妳剛剛不是已經餵過一次了，為什麼還要再餵一次呢？」

母親聽了以後，覺得事情有蹊蹺，趕緊察看小女嬰。她赫然發現小女嬰已經死了，而且身體內臟被吃得一乾二淨，肚子裏只剩下一堆稻草。

原來阿里嘎該變成母親的模樣，騙過大女兒，早就把小女嬰害死了。

還發生另一件怪事，部落裡一戶人家，丈夫像往常一樣出外捕魚，妻子在家做家事，等待丈夫歸來。這一天，丈夫似乎回來得特別早，而且帶回豐富的漁獲。

全家人津津有味地吃完鮮美的海鮮，夫妻倆滿足的倒頭熟睡。不知睡了多久，妻子突然被外頭敲門的聲音驚醒；她起身應門，發現自己的丈夫就站在門口，而原先睡在身旁的丈夫早已不見蹤影。

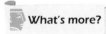

What's more?

巴力克（Pazik）：山名，即今日花蓮市區的美崙山。

捕魚（mitafukud，米達福故德）：阿美族人擅捕魚，一般用八卦網撒網，部分則用定置魚簍或射魚的技巧。

漁獲（futing，福定）：阿美族沒有特別區分何種人吃何種魚。

聚會所（集會所）（talu'an，達魯安）：聚會所為男子階級成員的聚集地方，同時也是部落的行政、教育以及軍事機構。

事後回想，他們斷定這應當也是那會法術的巨人阿里嘎該做的。

像這樣的事情層出不窮，讓族人感到非常害怕。

部落長老們為了不讓事情再發生，決定將所有的小孩集中在聚會所裡，由青年幹部們照顧、保護。婦女不管待在家中，還是出門，一律結伴而行，絕對不單獨行動。

這些防範措施，果然嚇阻了巨人阿里嘎該，令他一時無法侵擾阿美族人。可是，這樣做並不能永遠阻止巨人阿里嘎該。

巨人阿里嘎該因為很久沒有吃東西，餓得很難受，乾脆把右手從聚會所的屋頂伸進去，要抓小孩來吃。幸好聚會所內有青年幹部保護，巨人阿里嘎該不但沒有吃到小孩，右手臂反而被砍斷。斷了手臂的巨人阿里嘎該並未因此遠離，他在山上砍下一根樹幹，施法將樹幹變成自己的手臂。

長老們認為必須徹底消滅巨人阿里嘎該，大頭目巴力克召集所有部落裏的青年，以年齡分成好幾個階層，巴力克再從中選出兩支勇士隊，分別命名為拉利基和力固拉。

出發前一個月，兩支勇士隊分別接受長跑、短跑、野外求生以及射箭等戰技訓練，過程既嚴格又艱辛。完成訓練後，兩支隊伍靜候長老的命令。

長老一聲令下，勇士們出發了，抵達巴力克山與巨人阿里嘎該作殊死戰。驍勇善戰的勇士們本來還佔上風，但沒多久，巨人阿里嘎該施展法術，勇

 What's more?

長老（mato'asay，馬度阿賽）：是部落的最高決策成員。

大頭目（kakitaan，嘎基達安）：早期阿美族部落大都由長老會議做決策，再交由年齡階層執行。

拉利基（Lalikit）、力固拉（Likuda）：都是一種舞蹈名稱，僅在豐年祭時組成。

士們無法抵擋，傷亡慘重。阿美青年不論火攻或箭射，都不能傷及巨人阿里嘎該一根汗毛。

於是，勇士隊領袖卡浪下令撤退。攻擊行動無功而返，令卡浪非常懊惱，不知該如何才好。有一天，卡浪因為太疲倦，迷迷糊糊地躺在一塊石頭上睡著了。

睡夢中，卡浪聽到海神說：「只要將祭祀用的布隆拿來使用，就可以抵擋阿里嘎該的法術。」

卡浪醒來，將海神的指示告訴長老們，並決定一試。族人開始製作布隆，準備與巨人阿里嘎該再次決戰。

對決當天，卡浪命令每一個勇士帶上布隆。果然，巨人阿里嘎該面對身上掛著布隆的勇士們，法術頓時失靈，很快就被打敗了。

戰敗的巨人阿里嘎該往海上逃走，消失得無影無蹤。

此後，阿美族人雖然過著平靜的生活，但是，大家仍不敢掉以輕心，每年都將訓練部落青年，做為阿美族豐年祭的主要活動。同時，為了感謝海神，也舉行海祭，以紀念這一段恩情。

Where did it come from?
本故事採集自德興部落（花蓮市國富里）。

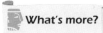
What's more?

勇士隊（kapah，軋巴）：由青年階層中的中堅份子所組成。

布隆（Porong）：做成的形狀像箭一般，前端用蘆葦捲綁成箭矢狀，通常用來做為祭祀的用具。

豐年祭、海祭（Milisin，米立信）：海祭為Mila'dis（米臘立斯），請詳見部落百寶盒：阿美族的重要祭典。

女人國歷險記

漂流多日的馬糾糾昏睡醒來後，發現身邊全是女人；讓他受驚害怕的是，她們要把他養肥後吃掉。幸虧得到送飯少女的同情以及大鯨魚的相助，順利逃回故鄉。

因此他每年都到海邊，獻上祭品，紀念這段恩情；這也是阿美族海祭習俗的由來之一。

從前有一個叫做馬糾糾的青年，平日非常勤奮工作。這一天，馬糾糾如同平常一樣來到田裡，忽然間下起滂沱大雨。

雨下得太大，河水暴漲起來，滾滾洪水快速向陸面逼近，馬糾糾也被沖到海上。幸好，他抱住一根木頭，才不至於被淹死。

不知過了多久，馬糾糾漂流到一個不知名的島嶼。島嶼的景象和他的部落看起來很像，他便往島上走，看看是否有部落存在。

馬糾糾走了好久，沒有發現人煙。走著走著，感覺累了，他便在樹下休息，小睡一番。恍惚間，他彷彿聽到一大群人走路的聲音，並且朝他的方向過來。

馬糾糾突然驚醒，發現身旁已經圍繞著許多拿著刀子和長矛的人，更令他奇怪的是：這些人全部都是女人！

當中一位長得非常漂亮的女人說：「這是什麼動物，怎麼以前都沒有見過？不過看起來好像很好吃的樣子。」馬糾糾聽了，害怕極了。

馬糾糾原想逃跑時，卻被女人們發覺了，便被綑綁起來，帶回她們居住的地方。

馬糾糾被綁到這些女人的部落後，才發現她們的部落沒有男人，所有的工作都由女人承擔。她們生育後代的方法很特別，想生小孩的人只要到部落附近的一座高山上，迎著風將雙臂打開，微風吹過雙臂，小孩子便會從腋下生出來。

就因為這樣，所以她們不需要男人，也從來沒有看過男人。

馬糾糾被她們關在離部落有一段距離的一個大籠子裡，不久，來了一位更

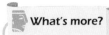

What's more?

頭目：阿美族的頭目沒有性別限制。

漂亮的女人，周圍的人似乎非常尊敬她。馬糾糾心想：「她應該是這一個部落的頭目吧！」

女頭目看著馬糾糾說：「這隻動物看起來好像非常鮮美，不過就是太瘦了。把他養肥一點，吃起來比較可口。」她對身旁的人交待完畢後，便轉身離去。馬糾糾聽了還來不及求饒，女頭目和他的隨從早已不知去向。

第二天起，吃飯時間一到，就會有一位少女送飯來，菜餚非常豐盛。馬糾糾不敢吃太多，因為他害怕變胖，會被她們殺來吃。

馬糾糾想逃脫，可是籠子太堅固，根本無法做到。後來，馬糾糾發現送飯來的都是同一位少女，而且看起來很善良，他決心向少女求救。

有一天，少女像往常一樣送飯來，馬糾糾趁機開口，請求少女幫忙。

少女聽馬糾糾開口說話，十分訝異，才知道馬糾糾原來也是人，因而答應他的請求。

少女返回部落前，將身上的刀子解下來給馬糾糾。不過，馬糾糾並沒有立即逃脫，等到黑夜，才用刀子將籠子破壞，往海邊方向逃跑。

到達海邊時，馬糾糾發現很多火把追來，心中非常著急，不知該如何是好。忽然間海上浮出一隻大鯨魚，並開口對馬糾糾說：「我是少女的朋友，她要我來救你回家。」

馬糾糾慌張地跳上鯨背，大鯨魚迅速游向大海。追趕的女人們雖然使勁丟矛、射箭，甚至試圖划船接近，幸好大鯨魚游泳的速度快，追兵越來越落在後面；最後馬糾糾總算順利逃脫，才不至於成為女頭目桌上的佳餚。

大鯨魚游到馬糾糾的故鄉，馬糾糾爬下來還來不及道謝，大鯨魚就轉身游進海裡。

回到部落後，馬糾糾才發現他已經離開好幾十年了；部落中認識他的人已經不多。他為了感謝少女和大鯨魚，每年都到海邊獻上檳榔、糯米糕和酒來紀念他們。這也是阿美族海祭習俗的由來之一。

Where did it come from?
本故事採集自德興部落（花蓮市國富里）。

What's more?

火把（satotom，沙度敦）：早期的阿美族人是用稻草捆成一束，再點燃火焰。

糯米糕（torom，都輪）：用糯米打製而成。

酒（'epah，兒霸喝）：據聞早期是由部落最純潔的少女將唾液混合小米製成。

檳榔（'icep，依芝普）：視檳榔為貴重物品主要為阿美族、卑南族、排灣族、魯凱族，其他各族是晚近才受影響。檳榔對阿美族來說是祭儀貢品，也是交友聯誼必需品。

螃蟹人的秘密

沒見過有人一出生就是人頭蟹身，而且長不大。他的父母不但沒有拋棄他，還幫他娶了媳婦。

在一個奇妙的情境下，螃蟹人突然變成正常人且英俊高大；感謝老天眷顧，這家人從此過著平順的生活。不過，長得特別快的遺傳基因還存在阿美族人的血液裡呢！

從前台灣東海岸住著一對阿美族夫婦，以捕魚和採集其他海產維生。這對夫妻生下一個男嬰，只是這個男嬰長得異於常人，人頭蟹身，讓他們很難過。

夫婦倆原本想把男嬰丟到海裡，讓他自生自滅；但終究是自己的小孩，不忍丟棄。

過了幾個月，未滿周歲的男嬰突然開口向父母說：「謝謝媽媽、爸爸把我留下，將來我一定要成為真正的人。」父母親聽了非常驚喜，決定要好好的扶養他長大。

螃蟹人平常不吃東西，睡覺時拿香蕉葉當棉被來蓋，有時候也會到海邊幫父母撿拾木柴。

有一天，螃蟹人竟然要求父母親幫他找一位妻子，父母親十分為難，便對螃蟹人說：「孩子啊！不是我不幫你，而是怕別人不願意啊！」

最後，經不起螃蟹人再三要求，父母親只好在鄰近部落為他找妻子。好不容易，終於有個女孩願意嫁給螃蟹人。可是，女孩嫁過來之後，女孩卻一直見不到自己的丈夫。

女孩終於受不了了，就跟螃蟹人的父母抱怨說：「我已經嫁過來很久，也沒有犯過大錯，為什麼不讓我看一看我的丈夫呢？」

女孩因而堅持要離開，螃蟹人的父母沒有辦法，只好跟螃蟹人商量。「昨晚我夢見自己將成為真正的人，請把我用香蕉葉包起來，放在水井邊的水桶裡；也請你們無論如何一定要將我的妻子再多留一夜。」螃蟹人對父母說。

What's more?

香蕉葉（papah no pawli，巴巴努巴力）：在花蓮北部阿美族部落裡，祭司有時會使用香蕉葉做為法器，以利法術和儀式的進行。

父母聽了螃蟹人的懇求之後，便對媳婦說：「妳想走，我們也沒有辦法留住你。這樣吧！我們到山上弄一些山產，好讓妳帶回去做紀念。」就這樣把媳婦多留了一天。

第二天一早，女孩到水井旁取水洗臉時，發現水桶裡有一個奇怪的小男孩。當陽光照射過來時，小男孩頓時長大成為一個英勇的男子。

螃蟹人將情況一五一十告訴驚恐不已的女孩。這時女孩才知道在水桶中的小男孩原來就是自己的丈夫，也才理解父母不讓她與丈夫相見的原因。

過了一段時間，螃蟹人夫婦生下了一男一女。

有一天，螃蟹人夫婦要出外工作，吩咐女兒要好好照顧弟弟，女兒乖巧地答應了。她小心的搖著搖籃，在弟弟睡著之後，才出去和鄰家的小孩玩。

沒多久，小女孩回家看顧弟弟，發現家門口有一位陌生的男子在東張西望。

小女孩不等這位陌生男子開口，就問了一連串的問題：「你是誰？」「要做什麼？」男子誠懇地說：「姊姊，我是你的弟弟啊！或許妳不相信，但是妳可以問一些家裡的事情，看我知不知道。」

小女孩衝到搖籃旁，發現弟弟已經不見了。她非常驚訝，決定考一考這位陌生男子。然而不管她問什麼，男子對家中種種都能對答如流。

儘管如此，小女孩還是半信半疑。這時候，螃蟹人夫婦回來了。小女孩將情形告訴父母，爸媽笑著說：「沒錯，他的確是妳的弟弟！」原來螃蟹人家庭非常特別，每一代總會有長得特別快的小孩呢！

Where did it come from?
本故事採集自德興部落（花蓮市國富里）。

部落百寶盒 ││ 傳授哈「原」秘笈，搖身變成阿美通

一、台灣花東的阿美族

阿美族人居住在花蓮、台東的縱谷及海岸地帶，分佈範圍非常廣。

早期日本學者將阿美族以地理位置為分類依據，有「三分法」與「五分法」等等分類方式：

「三分法」是指北部群、中部群與南部群。其中，北部群與中部群大致以花蓮縣壽豐鄉為分界點；中部群與南部群則以台東縣池上鄉為界。

「五分法」又將中部群以海岸山脈為界，分為秀姑巒阿美與海岸阿美；並把南部群中分佈於台東縣的稱為卑南阿美，分佈於屏東縣的叫恆春阿美，所以共有南勢阿美、秀姑巒阿美、海岸阿美、卑南阿美，以及恆春阿美五類。

另外，語言分類法和五分法大致相同，但另將撒奇萊雅和太巴塱—馬太鞍獨立出來，各自成一類。

▶ 阿美族的分類體系表

三分法	五分法	語言分類法	部　落
北部群	南勢阿美	撒奇萊雅	例如德興部落、國福部落、馬力雲部落等。
		南勢阿美	例如荳蘭部落、薄薄部落、里漏部落、七腳川部落等。
中部群	秀姑巒阿美	太巴塱馬太鞍	例如太巴塱部落、馬太鞍部落等。
	海岸阿美	中部群	例如玉里部落、鶴岡部落、瑞北部落、奇美部落、豐富部落、豐濱部落、大港口部落等。
南部群	卑南阿美	南部群	例如成功部落、馬蘭部落、都蘭部落等。
	恆春阿美		

當然，以上所提供的分界原本就不易絕對區分，加上隨著人口的增加與部落間的遷移、互動，彼此的界線早已經漸漸模糊不清，大多數的部落已混居多種的系統人群。一般說來，仍以部落為依據來分類較為恰當，最能顯現阿美族各部落的個別特色和多樣性。

二、與自然共舞的六個部落

早期的阿美族分佈於花蓮、台東的縱谷以及海岸地帶，由北到南有著許多的部落，每個部落隨著天然環境的特質與差異，各富有自己的明顯特色。

▶ 里漏部落

位於花蓮北邊的里漏部落（位於花蓮縣吉安鄉），是目前阿美族存在最多祭司的部落。每年夏天豐年祭前夕，所有部落的祭司都會穿戴上整齊的傳統服飾，手拿法器，集體出巡到各部落為族人祈福驅邪，壯觀的場面讓人不由得肅然起敬。

▶ 荳蘭部落

荳蘭部落（位於花蓮縣吉安鄉）目前仍保有八年一次的年齡階層晉級儀式（詳見「部落百寶盒：勇士的成長之路」）。新晉級人員在凌晨五點左右，要以跑步方式到達會場（路途至少有五、六公里遠），到達會場後，還要手牽手開始舞蹈，展現出活力與精神；平常若沒好好培養體力，恐怕很難完成這項儀式。

▶ 太巴塱部落

在中部最有名的部落要算是太巴塱部落（位於花蓮縣光復鄉），「太巴塱」的意思為「白色的螃蟹」，相傳太巴塱的族人遷移至此時，當地有許多的白色螃蟹。太巴塱是目前阿美族人口最多的部落，其保存的傳統文化也是最多的。尤其是每年的豐年祭往往進行三到五天，所有的儀式過程均按照古禮進行，同時附近部落的成員也會一起加入，參與豐年祭的總人數往往多達近千人，場面遠比其他部落盛大。

▶ 馬太鞍部落

鄰近的馬太鞍部落（位於花蓮縣光復鄉），保有完整的濕地環境，由濕地衍生的河祭與漁撈活動，充分顯示出阿美族早期與大自然結合為一體的生活智慧與和善活潑的個性。

▶ 宜灣部落

南邊就以台東成功的宜灣部落（位於台東縣成功鎮）最負盛名，除了保有豐富的傳統祭儀與風俗外，部落中的長老黃貴潮先生對於阿美族的文化記錄非常完備，因此黃先生常被尊稱為「阿美族的活字典」。讀者若有機會走一趟花東濱海公路，經過宜灣時，不妨停下腳步，除了欣賞美麗的風光之外，也可多停留以充分了解阿美族文化之美，絕對不虛此行。

▶ 都蘭部落

都蘭部落（位於台東縣東河鄉）位於阿美族傳說中的發源地——都蘭山山下，部落豐年祭特有的勇士舞，最具特色，由穿戴整齊傳統服裝的部落青年，手持花傘（早期是手持長矛，後因日本政府認為有危險性而改為持花傘），以上半身挺直，下半身單腳交互跳躍方式，進入豐年祭會場。

試試看，這種舞步很耗費體力，可不是常人能夠勝任的！

三、阿美族的重要祭典

早期台灣的原住民各族生活物資常取自於大自然，所以一切生活作息都能夠與大自然環境結合成一體，包括各項重要節慶也不例外。不過，快速工業化後的今天，阿美族的傳統祭儀也與各族一樣，漸漸開始轉變，甚至慢慢消失。目前阿美族仍然保留的一些歲時祭典，大致有豐年祭、河祭、海祭等。

▶ 歡樂歌舞慶豐年

豐年祭是阿美族目前各部落仍然保留的重要祭典。在水稻引進台灣以前，阿美族主要的作物以旱稻和小米為主，其收成時間大約國曆六月底至八月底左右，依照緯度的高低，由南而北依序成熟。豐年祭便是為了慶祝作物豐收而舉辦，所以阿美族各部落豐年祭的時間也是由台東往花蓮依序舉行，對阿美族來說這更是相當於新的一年的開始。

依慣例，每年的豐年祭確切日期是由部落長老偕同祭司視當年狀況決定的，舉行的時間大致上是三到七天，但現在因族人多半在外工作，而且請假不易，大部分的部落已逐漸把豐年祭縮短為一天，同時訂在週休二日，方便族人從外地趕回來參加。

在活動前，年齡組織的各級階層便展開豐年祭的準備事項，各家各戶都要準備阿美族的傳統菜餚，例如籐心、都輪（torom，糯米糕）、哈克哈克（hakhak，糯米糰）、麵包果、山蘇芽、黃麻湯等，小米酒更是不可或缺的飲料。當夜幕降臨大地，豐年祭舞蹈正式展開，大家穿著整齊的傳統服裝，到了祭典場地，手牽著手，依照各年齡階層圍成一圈，剛開始由男子隨著領唱者與帶領跳舞者，以不斷變化的舞步，揭開豐年祭的序幕；到了後半段時間，女子才開始陸陸續續的加入，這時便進入豐年祭的另一個活動高潮，也就是情人之夜的時段，是年輕未婚族人找尋情人或伴侶的最佳時機了。

▶ 祈求海神、河神來庇佑

除了豐年祭外，因為阿美族是台灣原住民族最會利用漁獲資源的民族，因此河祭與海祭也是阿美族重要的祭典，舉行的時間在豐年祭之前，象徵一年的結束。

在花蓮市附近的阿美族部落，都會舉行海祭，日期由長老開會決定。海祭當天凌晨四點左右，長老與祭司們在海邊開始祭拜海神，然後由年齡階級最高一級的青年悄悄下海捕魚；接著，再由其他階層下水捕魚，所有人捕到的漁獲都不能帶回家，必須上繳給長老，統一由長老依貢獻大小分配給族人。分配時並預留一部分當場煮熟做為聚餐的食物，餐後再舉行跑步等體育活動。最後由低階的年齡階級清理場地，結束全部的活動。

現在，秀姑巒溪流域的阿美族各部落大致還保留著河祭，花蓮北部與花東海岸靠海的各部落，則保有海祭。不管是河祭或海祭，一樣都是祈求阿美族人在捕魚時能受到河川、海洋神祇保佑，既平安又漁獲豐收。

四、絢爛的傳統歌舞

一九九六年，亞特蘭大奧運的一支宣傳短片，引用了阿美族「飲酒歡樂歌」的旋律。這首在全世界發聲的歌曲出自台東縣馬蘭部落，由已去世的阿美族郭英男夫婦吟唱，聽來宛如置身高聳的海崖上，感受洶湧的波濤陣陣拍打岸邊，令人盪氣迴腸。

▶ 阿美族人天生好歌喉

阿美族有豐富的傳統歌謠，配合著曼妙的舞步，織畫出五彩繽紛的景象，這就是阿美族人活潑開朗的主要動力，其中最精采的就是每年各部落舉行的「豐年祭」。豐年祭所表現的歌曲，採用領唱與和腔（類似答唱）的方式，連接緊密，節奏強烈，旋律優美。

阿美族的歌曲音樂種類大致可以分為虛詞歌謠與實詞歌謠，虛詞歌謠包括豐年祭歌、標題歌曲（類似外國交響樂的樂曲，純粹以意境為主）、歡宴歌曲，這些歌曲並沒有歌詞（「嘿呀歐嗨泱」並非實質意義的歌詞），純粹屬於意境的歌謠，必須由心神去領會；實詞歌謠即為有實質意義歌詞存在的歌謠，其包含的項目很多，凡是有歌詞的歌曲都算。

雖然阿美族的舞蹈與歌謠緊密結合，但他們有時候只會唱歌謠而不舞蹈，卻絕不會只舞蹈而沒有歌謠的配合。一般來說，阿美族的舞蹈可以分為豐年祭使用的舞蹈與平日歡樂慶典使用的舞蹈，兩者不能相混淆，因此豐年祭使用的舞蹈絕不可以於一般場合使用，而一般場合使用的舞蹈，也不可以使用在正式的豐年祭慶典上。

▶ 壯觀又變化萬千的舞蹈

阿美族的舞蹈形式大致分為群舞與獨舞，舞步因部落不同而有差異。群舞多在大型場合使用，一般豐年祭的舞蹈屬於群舞，且雙手互與他人相牽，形成「一條龍」形狀，舞步由帶頭的人隨歌曲不同而改變，時而圍圓圈，時而相互穿梭，因此阿美族豐年祭的舞蹈十分壯觀而又變化萬千，足以使觀賞者眼花撩亂；一般場合的舞蹈則有群舞與獨舞兩種，群舞多半雙手不互牽，此時配合著歌曲，可以展現出個人的舞蹈風格，表現出另一種美。總而言之，阿美族不管男女老少，都可以隨性唱出一曲或舞出一段舞蹈來。

五、勇士的成長之路

在阿美族的傳統社會中，有一項制度是阿美族非常重要的，那就是「年齡階級」。當男孩子到了十三、四歲的時候，母親會將他送到聚會所，開始接受三年預備訓練，訓練結束後接受「成年禮」儀式。

▶ 經成年洗禮擔當大任

阿美族男孩子接受祭司祈福保佑後，經過長老與領導階級（mama no kapah 麻罵努軋巴）的訓話，了解到成年所應盡的義務後，由長老或領導階級以籐或竹在臀部上象徵性鞭打一下，才可以正式進入「年齡階級」。這個訓練可以說是集合了政治、軍事、教育等功能，也可以說是阿美族男子成為智仁勇兼備勇士的必經過程。

至於女孩子的成年禮則是由家族最年長的婦女主持儀式，與男孩子比較起來，沒有太多的儀式活動，只要經過主持人認可，便表示這個女孩子已進入成年，開始承擔成年人的義務。

▶ 年齡階級具有政治、軍事、教育功能

在政治上，依年齡可以分成好幾個階層，並且再按各部落人口多寡，有的二至三歲、也有五至八歲為一個階層，低階層的人必須完全接受、服從較上階層的命令。當長老會議（由部落全部的長老組成，頭目則由長老裡互推）做出決定後，會交代給年齡階級的最高階層，也就是領導階級來執行，再依事情的性質分配給其他階級執行。

在軍事上，年齡階級是主要的部落武力組成，因此進入年齡階級的青年，必須在成年時接受體力、競技的訓練，例如負重、跑步、射箭等，同時也必須完全服從上一階級的命令。

在教育方面，部落也往往透過年齡階級在聚會、工作、訓話等活動下，例如捕魚漁具的製作、採籐與編織的方法、野菜的判斷與烹煮等等，一一將部落的歷史、技能以及生活知識傳授給下一階層，達到傳承的功能。

▶ 年齡階級的命名方式

正如同每個階級都會有不同的命名，每個部落的命名制度也有所不同，大致

可以分為「襲名制」和「創名制」。

所謂「襲名制」就是年齡階級中，每個階級的名字固定，依序輪迴使用，例如花蓮縣壽豐鄉水璉部落（Ciwidian，基威立安）第一級「拉拉烏」（rarawo）即為基石之意。

「創名制」是依據當時組成此階層時所發生的重大發生事件來命名，例如花蓮縣豐濱鄉大港口部落階級名「拉荷蘭」（raholan），意思是漢人大量遷移到東部。

雖然隨著社會的變遷，現代政府機構、軍隊以及學校完全取代了年齡階級的功能，不過阿美族敬老尊賢、長幼有序的倫理觀念，如今依然透過年齡階級的制度，繼續傳承給每個阿美族青年。

▶ **阿美族年齡階級的職責及分工表**（以花蓮縣壽豐鄉水璉部落為例）

組名	譯義	級職名	任務
rarawo（拉拉烏）	基石	makateloc（馬嘎德陸茲）	作戰前鋒，工作主力
alamay（阿喇買）	魚鱗雲	pa'afangay（巴阿伐耐）	支援站立，協助工作
aladiwas（阿喇力娃斯）	神壺	mitadoroay（米達魯陸愛）	指導工作，實質監督
alafangas（阿喇發那斯）	枯連樹	mitalifanaay（米達力發那愛）	督導
matafok（馬達傅克）	自動自發	mitelongay（米得陸耐）	領導中心
ma'orad（馬歐臘）	春雨	misimaway（米西馬外）	顧問、留守
maorac（馬歐臘茲）	耐旱植物	pahololay（巴荷陸賴）	退休
maoway（馬歐外）	黃藤	maroay（馬魯愛）	自由之身（安靜的坐著）
alemet（阿樂麼）	猴子樹	kalas（軋臘斯）	最受尊敬的長老

阿美族年齡階級除了有以上所說的「襲名制」和「創名制」組名區別外，另有固定的級職名，由表中的級職名便可以得知各個工作內容。

六、檳榔牽起好姻緣

阿美族是一個完全的母系社會，女方在家中的地位非常重要，家中的主要家長是最年長的婦女，而男方在家中則附屬於女方，家中的所有財產以及孩子都屬於母親，只有女人才有權力處置家中的所有一切。

▶ 情投意合來完婚

豐年祭儀式也是男女表達情意最主要的機會，在豐年祭的最後一個晚上，也就是情人之夜，男方為了得到女方的注意，會非常賣力藉跳舞表現剛強英姿；女方如果屬意，就將檳榔置放在男方的情人袋中。有的部落也盛行男女雙方如果情投意合，男方會到山中砍拾最好的木材送給女方；女方也會到男方家中幫忙家務，以取得男方母親的好感。

根據早期流傳下來的慣例，當雙方決定要結婚時，準新娘必須準備聘禮（sapakatim紗巴軋訂姆），並邀請女方的親友共進晚餐；然後，由準新娘與兄弟姊妹攜帶聘禮到男方家中，將聘禮送給男方，便返回家中。第二天中午，女方親屬會準備豐盛酒餚，宴請男方家中成員，宴會結束後，賓客一一離開；再換男方當天回請女方家屬成員到家中吃晚飯。飯後，女方賓客告辭，新娘也偕同新郎返回女方家，新郎開始在女方家中過夜，完成結婚儀式。

▶ 女方「娶」男方到家中

當雙方適應一段時間均滿意對方時，女方會將男方「娶」到家中，也就是說，男方必須到女方家居住。男方在女方家要每天很早就起床，到田裡耕種或刻苦耐勞工作，若是好吃懶做，女方會將男方的衣物放置門外，表示解除婚姻。當男方看到自己的衣物在門外時，也會知趣的離開，男女雙方便又各自找尋自己的婚姻伴侶。

現今隨著工業化生活以及主流社會的影響，阿美族的婚禮開始轉向由男方主導的父系嫁娶婚，傳統的阿美族婚禮已經漸漸消失不見了。

七、天賜多樣的原味食物

早期的阿美族人大多居住在現在花蓮、台東兩個地方，少數則遷移到屏東恆春地區。雖然有些阿美族的部落並不靠海，但是對於捕魚的技術卻是同樣的熟稔。

▶ 阿美族人是捕魚高手

我們常常可以聽到阿美族人說：「只要有水的地方，就會有阿美族人的存在。」的確，阿美族的捕魚技巧是台灣原住民族中最為有名的，在阿美族的家庭裡，經常可以看到竹編的圓柱形魚筌、魚簍、魚簾以及八卦網；更可以在一些阿美族的傳統技藝比賽裡看到灑八卦網競技，從大家灑網的技巧如同天女散花般的美麗，就可以想像阿美族人的捕魚技術有多麼高超了！

▶ 野菜烹調一極棒

阿美族人在認識野菜方面的知識，也是其他台灣原住民族比不上的。阿美族人一般認識的野菜種類多達百種以上，而烹調出來的野菜菜餚，美味總是讓人食指大動。介紹幾道阿美族人的風味餐吧，先來水煮山蘇、醃山豬肉、涼拌海帶當冷盤，過貓炒小魚、爆炒林投樹心、麵包果炒肉絲等是香噴噴的熱菜，山豬肉燉檳榔心、籐心燉排骨、烤鵪鶉等大菜上桌，再來小米飯糰、竹筒飯、小米糕當主食，嘴饞時吃炒太巴塱豆，喝一口小米酒，這一餐真是豐盛又美味。

近年來，隨著社會大眾對健康的重視，許多人發現食用阿美族的野菜，可以增加對某些疾病的抵抗力，阿美族人也不吝惜的提供許多傳統的野菜，在花蓮吉安的黃昏市場擺設有許多攤位供人們選購。大家有興趣的話，不妨到花蓮的黃昏市場走一趟，除了可以認識許多阿美族人常吃的野菜外，同時也可以選購一些菜餚，帶回家中烹調；既可以享受美食，又可以增進身體健康，真是一舉數得。

造訪部落　部落藏寶圖，來挖阿美寶

看過了阿美族的神話與傳說故事，想不想跟著福通和莎樣一起爬通往天上的梯子（位在花蓮縣舞鶴台地上）；到花東海岸尋訪螃蟹人的身影，吹著海螺呼喚海神；和阿美族勇士合力奮戰，擊退巨人阿里嘎該？！

阿美族在台灣原住民族中，人口最多（註），分佈在花蓮、台東的縱谷及海岸地帶。現在，透過這份精心編製的「阿美族部落文化導覽圖」，陪伴身歷其境，盡情挖掘部落文化寶藏，保證不虛此行。

當然，造訪部落時更不能錯過阿美族豐富的祭儀活動，像是五、六月的「海祭」或「河祭」，七、八月份的「豐年祭」。心動想要行動之前，最好先確定時間及地點，可與花蓮、台東各鄉鎮公所原住民行政課或東管處遊客中心查詢。

洽詢電話：
- 花蓮縣政府原住民行政局輔導行政課　電話：03-8234531
- 台東縣政府原住民行政局教育文化課　電話：089-320112
- 觀光局東管處遊客服務中心　電話：089-841520分機1601
  （網址：http://www.eastcoast-nsa.gov.tw）

註：依2021年10月原民會資料及21.5萬人

阿美族
文化導覽圖

族語開口說 **入境隨俗的阿美語**

你好！
ngay ho no miso.
乃　候 努 米索

你好！
ngay ho no miso.
乃　候 努 米索

請問貴姓大名？
cima ko ngangan iso?
基麻 古 那難　　伊書

我的名字叫做馬輝。
ci mayaw ko ngangan kako.
基 馬罐　古 那難　　嘎古

請問你住何方？
icuwa ko loma iso?
芋諸娃 古 盧麻 伊書

我的家在荳蘭部落（花蓮縣吉安鄉）。
i natawran ko loma kako.
依 納豆蘭　　古　盧麻 嘎古

這是什麼？
o maam koni?
烏 麻安　古尼

這是糯米糕。
o torom koni.
烏 都輪　古尼

你們午餐都吃些什麼？
o maan ko dateng no namoa a malahok?
烏 麻安 古 拉鄧　努 那姆 阿 馬拉候幹

我們的午餐菜餚有野菜和豬肉。
o tatokem ato titi　ko dateng no niyam.
烏 大度根 阿杜 地地 古 拉鄧 努　　那姆

你們的部落是什麼時候舉行豐年祭？
ano hacuwa a milisin ko niyaro' namo?
阿努 哈祖哇 阿 米立信 古 尼亞路 那姆

我們的部落在八月左右舉行豐年祭。
i saka falo a folad ko ilisin no niyaro' kami.
伊 沙軋 發喇 阿 福拉曰 古 伊立信 努 尼亞路 嘎米

我可以參加你們的豐年祭舞蹈嗎？
manga'ay kako a mikapot a malikoda how?
驛乃愛　　嘎古 阿 米軋布 阿 馬力古臘 好

我們可以一起來參加豐年祭舞蹈。
manga'ay to malakapot kita a malikoda.
驛乃愛　　度 馬拉軋布 基大 阿 馬力古臘

我真的很喜歡你的部落。
tada maolah kako to niyaro' namo?
蓬臘 馬烏辣 嘎古 度 尼亞路 那姆

感謝你的到來。
miahowid kako to tataniay iso.
米阿侯維 嘎古 度 達帶泥 伊書

很高興能見到你。
malip ahak ko faloco' a ma'araw kamo.
馬力巴 哈克 古 發露祖 阿 馬阿落 嘎姆

很高興能再次相見。
tada malip ahak ko faloco' a maso'araw kita.
達臘 馬力巴 哈克 古 發露祖 阿 馬阿落　　基達

那麼我就回去了。
minokay to kako.
米努蓋　度 嘎古

祝一路順風。
na'onen ko rakat.
那歐嫩　古 喇尬

族語開口說　**阿美族稱謂的介紹**

akong	阿公	阿公（花蓮的說法由河洛語發音）
faki'	發基	阿公（台東的說法）
mamo	麻目	阿媽
ina	伊娜	媽媽
mama、wama、ama	麻罵、瓦罵、阿罵	爸爸（三者均可使用）
fayi	發意	阿姨和姑姑
faki'	發基	伯伯、叔叔、舅舅
kaka to fafahiyan	嘎嘎 度 發發意央	姊姊
safa to fafahiyan	沙發 度 發發意央	妹妹
kaka to fa'inayan	嘎嘎 度 發意那央	哥哥
safa to fa'inayan	沙發 度 發意那央	弟弟

學習加油站　**本書漢語與阿美語名詞對照表**

故事01：種田的陀螺

用漢字拼讀	阿美語	漢語名詞
法伊納央	fa'inayan	男子
福杜滋	Votoc	男子名
莎法	Savak	女子名
法法伊央	fafahiyan	女子
瑪拉拉姆萊	mararamoday	夫妻
娃娃	wawa	嬰兒、小孩子的統稱
拿拉拉扎南	Nararacanan	地名，在花蓮港附近
福通	Votong	男子名
古露米	Kurumi	女子名
莎樣	Sayan	女子名
邦查	Pangcah	人；花蓮地區阿美族自稱
阿米斯	Amis	北方人；台東阿美的稱法，已成為阿美族族名
撒奇萊雅	Sakizaya	阿美族之撒奇萊雅人
阿多莫	atomo	水桶
德封	tfon	水井
伊娜	ina	母親
卡雷	calay	繩子
德封挪福通	Tfon-no-Votong	福通池
麻蘇拿南	masunanam	求婚
巴達魯瑪	pataloma'	結婚
烏馬喝	omah	田
馬代雅	matayal	工作
米故里	mikoli	做工
阿祖祖勒	'acocol	陀螺
麻屋罵賀	maomah	開墾
軋賀基	kahcid	甜的
骯熱兒	'angrer	苦的
巴耐	panay	稻米

用漢字拼讀	阿美語	漢語名詞
哈發一	hafay	小米
沙立信	salisin	祭祀儀式
米德外	mitway	播粟祭
魯罵	loma'	家
布雅布伊	puyapuy	懷孕
軋軋拉央	kakarayan	天上或天空
軋娃兒	kawal	梯子
馬巴代	mapatay	死亡
福伊德魯	fitlok	肚子
麻魯能	malunen	鹿
發復伊	fafoy	豬
歐嫩兒	'oner	蛇
阿阿魯本	a'adopen	動物
掃叭	Sapad	位於舞鶴台地
馬伊富兒	Maifor	現今馬力雲部落

故事02：海神娶親

用漢字拼讀	阿美語	漢語名詞
懷露法絲	Vay-Rovas	女子名
法伊納央都娃娃	fa'inayan to wawa	兒子
法法伊央都娃娃	fafahiyan to wawa	女兒
麻軋巴哈	makapah	漂亮
芝希麗蘭	Cisiringan	女子名
里壓日	riyay	海邊
卡非特	Kafit	海神
不露兒	polol	籃子
軋荷納耐	kahngangay	紅色
竺故兒	cokor	手杖
達拉瓦烙	Tarawadaw	相傳位於現在秀姑巒溪出海口附近
麻臘日 阿 竺故兒	marad a cokor	鐵棒
軋蘭姆	karam	法術
基軋瓦賽	cikawasay	祭司

故事03：巨人阿里嘎該

用漢字拼讀	阿美語	漢語名詞
達達阿克 阿 黨姆老	tata'ak a tamdaw	巨人
巴力克	Pazik	山名； 今花蓮市美崙山
阿里嘎該	Alikakay	阿美族傳說中 巨人的名字
砂娃臘	sawada'	內臟
迪任兒	tireng	身體
迪亞日	tiyad	肚子
阿希秀	'asisiw	稻草
米達福故德	mitafukud	捕魚
福定	futing	漁獲
達魯安	talu'an	聚會所（集會所）
馬度阿賽	mato'asay	長老
馬馬努軋巴	mama no kapah	青年幹部
法拉宏恩	fadahong	屋頂
軋娃難	kawanan	右
法拉納兒	fadangal	手臂
魯度克	lotok	山上
基朗	kilang	樹幹、樹木、 木頭的說法相同
嘎基達安	kakitaan	大頭目
巴力克	Pazik	男子名
拉利基	lalikit	阿美族的舞蹈名稱
力固達	likuda	阿美族的舞蹈名稱
珠米蓋	cumikay	長跑
巴特兒	pa'ter	短跑
米巴納	mipana'	射箭
卡浪	Kalang	男子名
福各陸喝	fukloh	石頭
米福地	mifuti'	睡
樂麼日	lmed	夢
布隆	porong	祭祀用具之一
米立信	Milisin	豐年祭
米臘立斯	Mila'dis	海祭

故事04：女人國歷險記

用漢字拼讀	阿美語	漢語名詞
馬糾糾	Maciwciw	男子名
軋巴	kapah	青年
歐臘日	'orad	雨
阿路兒	'alo	河水
扎臘斯	cadas	洪水
斯拉兒	sra	陸地
軋水伊	kasoy	木柴
軋納臘	kanada'	島嶼
福怒斯	funus	刀子
伊勒資	'idoc	矛
法麗	fali	風
阿法拉	'afala	臂膀
軋立立安	kariri'an	腋下
達翁	ta'ong	尊敬
古立	kuri	瘦
孰述	so'so	肥
該映	kaying	少女
喇鄧恩	dateng	菜餚
軋巴 古 發陸族	kapah ko faloco'	善良
沙度敦	satotom	火把
伊術兒	'iso	大鯨魚
巴陸難	palunan	划船
都輪	torom	糯米糕
兒霸喝	'epah	酒
依芝普	'icep	檳榔

故事05：螃蟹人的秘密

用漢字拼讀	阿美語	漢語名詞
巴巴 努 巴力	papah no pawli	香蕉葉
軋放恩	kafang	棉被
軋浪	kalang	螃蟹人
法伊耐	fa'inay	丈夫
極臘兒	cidal	太陽
立軋特	likat	光
法伊納央阿沙伐	fa'inayan a safa	弟弟
福伊耀	fiyaw	鄰居
鼻納努央	pinanoyan	搖籃

部落百寶盒：台灣花東的阿美族

用漢字拼讀	阿美語	漢語名詞
紗故爾	Sakol	德興部落
嘎修修安	Kasyusyu-an	國福部落
馬伊富兒	Maifor	馬力雲部落
那荳蘭	Natawran	荳蘭部落
不布可	Popok	薄薄部落
里烙	Lidaw	里漏部落
基嘎書安	Cikasuan	七腳川部落
達發隆	Tafalon	太巴塱部落
發答安	Fata'an	馬太鞍部落
璞石閣	Posko	玉里部落
屋落	Olaw	鶴岡部落
達麥芽	Tamayan	瑞北部落
基維	Kiwit	奇美部落
丁那老	Tingalaw	豐富部落
法公	Fakong	豐濱部落
芝布蘭	Ceporan	大港口部落
麻烙落	Madawdaw	成功部落
法拉瑙	Falangaw	馬蘭部落
都蘭	Tolan	都蘭部落

部落百寶盒：阿美族的重要祭典

用漢字拼讀	阿美語	漢語名詞
哈克哈克	hakha	糯米糰

部落百寶盒：勇士成長之路

用漢字拼讀	阿美語	漢語名詞
麻罵努軋巴	mama no kapah	訓話儀式
基威立安	Ciwidian	水璉部落
拉拉烏	rarawo	基石
阿喇買	alamay	魚鱗雲
阿喇力娃斯	aladiwas	神壺
阿喇發那斯	alafangas	枯連樹
馬達傅克	matafok	自動自發
馬歐臘	ma'orad	春雨
馬歐臘茲	maorac	耐旱植物
馬歐外	maoway	黃籐
阿樂麼	alemet	猴子樹
馬嘎德陸茲	makateloc	作戰前鋒，工作主力
巴阿伐耐	pa'afangay	支援站立，協助工作
米達魯陸愛	mitadoroay	指導工作，實質監督
米達力發那愛	mitalifanaay	督導
米得陸耐	mitelongay	領導中心
米西馬外	misimaway	顧問、留守
巴荷陸賴	pahololay	退休
馬魯愛	maroay	自由之身（安靜的坐著）
軋臘斯	kalas	最受尊敬的長老

部落百寶盒：天賜多樣的原味食物

用漢字拼讀	阿美語	漢語名詞
紗巴軋訂姆	sapakatim	聘禮

造訪部落

用漢字拼讀	阿美語	漢語名詞
達故部灣	Takoboan	位於花蓮市 四維高中一帶
砂露	Sado	沙荖部落
沙阿尼灣	Sa'aniwan	宜灣部落

卑南族
Puyuma

▶小筆記▶

- 喜歡編花、戴花的民族。
- 為什麼開往台東的火車稱為普悠瑪號？
- 民歌教父胡德夫、金曲獎歌手張惠妹、陳建年、紀曉君、吳昊恩都有卑南血統。

・斯巴達式的會所制度讓人口稀少的卑南族曾雄霸花東。

・卑南遺址現為卑南文化公園，主要文物典藏於史前文化博物館。

・各種祭典串起文化傳承：猴祭、大獵祭、除草祭、海祭、收穫祭。

故事導讀　　Puyuma，團結的花環

卑南族是花東縱谷出海口沖積平原上的原住民族群，有八個主要部落。和許多台灣原住民族群一樣，「卑南」這個統稱的族名乃是日本時代殖民地政府強力認定的。其實原來的卑南族，比較是部落認同的。「卑南族」名稱族語的音讀應做「普悠瑪」（Puyuma），它指的是今天卑南族南王部落。近代以來，由於南王部落發展迅速，逐漸取代知本（katipul）部落的領導地位；所以，日本政府一來，就以南王部落的名稱統稱卑南族。

流傳在卑南族各部落的神話傳說，雖然有許多的相似性，但是由於各部落原本都是獨立自主的社會文化單元，因而也產生了不少個別性的差異，這種情況尤其以起源傳說為甚。知本系的起源神話，就和南王系的說法有著相當大的出入。

為了避免誤解，我們這裡所採錄的傳說故事，主要以南王部落的口傳為依據，所有的族語音讀也以南王音為準。這是我們首先應當要了解的。

〈都蘭山下的普悠瑪〉是南王部落的起源傳說，明確提到卑南族人大洪水之後，經由布肚兒（今蘭嶼島），輾轉來到都蘭山下遷移、繁衍的過程。我們在故事中，可以看到南王七個氏族聚落的形成與整合，也可以約略理解卑南族「會所制度」（palukuwan）的功能與價值。

〈神秘的月形石柱〉勾畫了一個殘忍、複雜的族群關係，這多少反映了卑南人在台東平原上的現實處境。土地、資源的爭奪，族群間的對立、矛盾，充分表現在故事的情節中。故事的主角那倆兄弟，其實隱喻了卑南族社會組織中的年齡階級，分別代表「少年會所」和「成年會所」，它們是卑南族社會的核心動力。藉由巫咒進行的血腥報復，一方面顯示卑南族會所制度嚴密、強悍的組織性力量，另一方面也證實了一般外族對卑南巫術靈力的恐懼。

布肚兒（蘭嶼）不只出現在卑南人的起源傳說中，也是卑南人小米（農業）移入的來源。故事敘述的過程雖略有不同，卻都非常生動有趣，我們從其中可以充分領略原住民古樸的幽默感。而整個〈感恩海祭的由來〉故事中所表現的精神，一方面是卑南人對蘭嶼人溯源感恩的宗教表達，另一方面也為卑南人進入台灣本島的路線留下了歷史的線索。

每年大獵祭（mangayaw）卑南族男子從獵區歸來，婦女們總是要編織一串又一串的花環，為自己的親人一圈又一圈的戴上，表示喜樂，也表示兩性和家族的團圓。〝murekesa ta〞，卑南語的意思是：「讓我們團結起來吧！」因祖先的花環，卑南族人緊緊的綁在一起，鮮花朵朵，成一個環，周而復始……。

Reader's Guide　　　Puyuma: Wreaths of Unity

Puyuma refers to an indigenous group located on the alluvial plain at the estuary of the Huadong Rift Valley, with eight main tribes. As with many indigenous groups in Taiwan, the collective name Beinan was used by the colonial Japanese government during its occupation of Taiwan. In fact, the original Puyuma is more tribal-identified. The pronunciation of the name "Puyuma" refers to the people of Nanwang village. In modern times, due to the relatively rapid development of Nanwang village tribe, it gradually replaced the leading position of the katipul tribe, and thus the Japanese government collectively referred to the Puyuma tribe by the name of the peoples of Nanwang village.

The stories presented in this series here are mainly based on the oral traditions of the Nanwang Puyuma, and the pronunciation of the Puyuma words is also based on the Nanwang pronunciation.

"Stories from the Puyuma of Dulan Mountain" is the creation story of the Nanwang Puyuma, a clear narration of how the people migrated through BuTul (Orchid Island) after the great flood. In the story, we can see the formation and integration of the settlements of the seven clans of the Southern King (Nanwang), and gain a rough understanding of the function and value of the Puyuma palukuwan or "meeting place".

"The Mysterious Crescent Stones" outlines tragic and complicated relations among different ethnic groups, a reflection of the reality for the Puyuma people on the pains of what is now Taitung County. The story illustrates the struggle for land and resources, and the antagonisms and contradictions between ethnic groups. The two brothers, the protagonists of the story, is actually a metaphor for the age distinctions in the Puyuma social organization, representing the "teen palukuwan" and the "adult palukuwan", which together constitute the core driving force of the Puyuma society. The bloody revenge carried out through witchcraft on the one hand shows the rigorous and powerful organization of the Puyuma palukuwan system, while it also confirms the general reputation among outsiders of the powerful Puyuma witchcraft.

BuTul not only appears in the creation story of Puyuma, but also as the source of the Puyuma millet agriculture. Although the stories vary slightly, they are all lively and interesting and can lead to a better appreciation of indigenous peoples' sense of humor. The spirit expressed in the story of "Origin of the Rites of Giving Thanks to the Sea " is both the heartfelt expression of the Puyuma people's tracing and gratitude to the people of BuTul for showing them the cultivation of millet, as well as a historical record of the Puyuma people's migration route to the island of Taiwan.

都蘭山下的普悠瑪

一場大洪水，淹沒了大地，卑南族的祖先帶著
族人搭上小舟，航向大海，要去尋找一個可以
安身立命、繁衍子孫的新家園。人類的強韌生
命力，在面臨困境時顯得耀眼動人，夢想也不
再遙不可及。

 What's more?

都蘭山（Tuangalan，都阿蘭或maiDangan，麥達安）：意思
是老人山或祖先山，被尊為聖山。

南王部落：1930年，日本政府統治台灣的時候，由於原居住
在卑南一帶的南王人發生傳染病，基於衛生以及疏緩外來人
口壓力的考量，部落的居民在日本政府的輔導下，遷到西邊
地名叫sakuban（沙古邦）的地方居住，而這個新聚落即為
現在的「南王部落」。另有一小群人遷移到台東市寶桑里，
就是這群人叫南王sakuban，而南王人還是喜歡用puyuma，
以示正統。

傳說中，都蘭山是卑南族南王部落人的祖先最早登陸和居住過的地方。

很久很久以前，南王部落人的祖先原本住在不知名的遙遠海外，由於世界發生了大洪水，洪水氾濫成災，淹沒了大地，人們無以為生。

於是，在男祖先阿都如冒和女祖先阿都如紹的帶領下，大約五、六戶人家，三十多位南王部落人，搭乘著木頭拼成的舟筏，乘風漂流，想要尋找一處可以居住的地方。

他們漂到一個叫做布肚兒的島上，傳說這個島就是現在的蘭嶼。當時島上已經有人居住了，但是他們還是留下來和島上的人一起生活。

不過，由於彼此的生活習慣不同，南王部落人常常和島上的人有衝突。阿都如冒和阿都如紹兩位祖先認為，布肚兒島不適合長久定居，於是決定離開。重新造舟、儲水、存糧，再往海上探險，希望能夠找到一個可以永遠安身立命的新天地。

離開布肚兒島後，他們划著小舟，在海上漫無目的地漂流了許多日子，都還看不見陸地。小舟隨波浪起伏搖晃，常常顛得大家很不舒服，而高掛天空的烈陽，也曬得人發暈，真是苦不堪言。可是為了不要再過寄人籬下的生活，南王部落人咬緊牙關苦撐，夢想新家園的建立。

有一天，他們忽然見到遠遠的海面，有一個形狀像翻過來的鍋子的陸地，大家都相當的雀躍、興奮，於是同心協力地用力往前划。划呀划，終於划到了岸邊，就在那裡登上了陸地。他們發現陸地上有花有草，有鳥有獸，很適合居住。這個登陸的地點，傳說就是現在的都蘭山。

在登上都蘭山以後，男祖先阿都如冒就用手抓起一把泥土扔到大海中，祈求海水能夠消退，果然海水因此降低了。

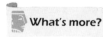
What's more?

布肚兒：指位於台東外海的蘭嶼。

當海水降退後，女祖先阿都如紹便說：「有平原了，女人們可以開始種植農作物。」於是他們就在那個地方定居下來了。

南王部落的祖先，在都蘭山一帶，大約住了幾百年，人口漸漸繁衍起來，人一多，田地就不夠使用，這下子該怎麼辦呢？

這個時候有人發現，在都蘭山腳下，有一個很大很大的平原，好像滿適合居住，而且能夠容納所有的人。

於是，大家開始商量遷移搬家的事宜。

一開始，有七位兄弟姐妹率先下山到大平原，並且在平原上各自選擇了最喜愛的地方，建造房子居住。後來，原本居住在山上的族人，見到他們遷到山下後，日子過得不錯，於是紛紛跟進遷下山來和他們一起同住，各自依照自己的喜愛或親疏遠近的關係，分別依附原先來的人，於是在平原上形成了七個不同的聚落。

從都蘭山往下遷徙的過程中，走到一處名叫阿邦安的地方時，有些老人們累得走不動了，就住在這個地底會湧出溫泉的地方，其他人則繼續前進。

抵達目的地後的親人，關心老人們的安危，時常派遣年輕人送米飯、食糧到阿邦安探視，這個習慣就成為日後南王部落舉行每年一度大獵祭時，必須先向都蘭山進行撒米祭獻儀式的由來。

定居在卑南平原上的人們，各自成立了一個個聚落，在平原上展開了他們

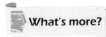

What's more?

七個不同的聚落：卑南族神話與傳說故事中的七個聚落分別為麥達達兒、巴巴都蘭、阿拉阿拉外、咕魯咕魯安、卡那巫肚、母奴奴弄、布吉特。

阿邦安：接近現在布農族居住的台東縣延平鄉榕山村，該地有溫泉湧出。

大獵祭（mangayaw，馬阿耀）：請參見部落百寶盒：年祭巡禮：大獵祭。

撒米祭拜儀式：請參見部落百寶盒：年祭巡禮：猴祭。

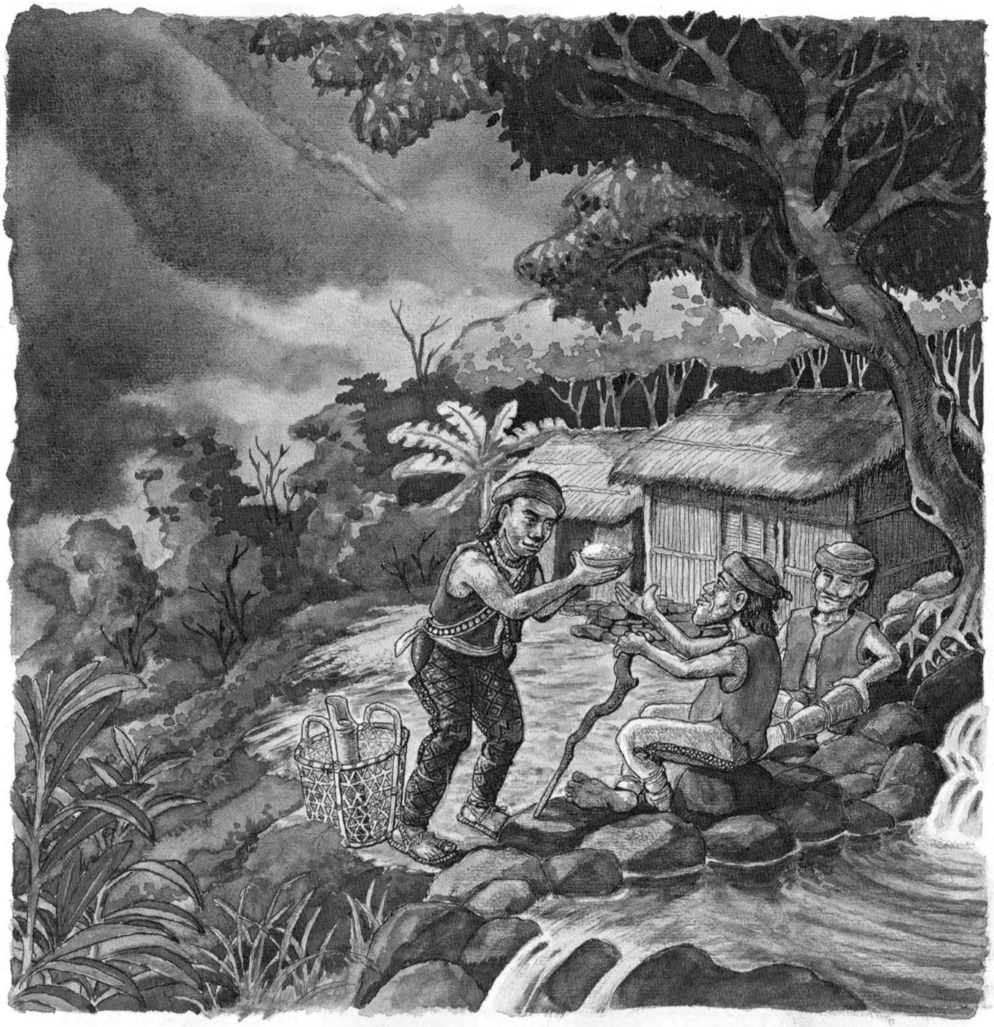

的生活，並靠著耕作和打獵維持生計。但是打獵前，他們仍然謹守團結的習慣，一定要先集合後，再一同出發打獵。

所以，就在大哥建立的麥達達兒聚落裡，蓋了一個集會用的建築，叫做巴拉冠，也就是現在的「會所」。其他兄弟見到會所很有用，於是就學大哥的做法，在自己的聚落裡建立屬於自己的會所。

會所，在卑南族人的社會中，是個很重要的處所，可說是男人生活的重心。會所就像現在的軍營，因為所有的成年男子，未結婚前都要住在這裡，隨時防犯敵人的來襲。會所又像學校，年輕的男子在這裡可以向老人家們學習各種知識。

後來，大家總覺得分散居住，力量不能夠集中，一旦敵人來犯時，難以自保。於是大家又一起商量，決定集中到麥達達兒，也就是大哥住的地方共同生活，互相照應。

為了紀念這種集合的行動，就用卑南族的古話「普悠瑪」相稱。後來，意味著集合團結的普悠瑪，逐漸成了現在卑南族南王部落的名字，日據時代更成為全族的名字。

Where did it come from?

本故事由台東市南王社區發展協會理事長陳光榮長老講述。

 What's more?

麥達達兒：卑南族神話與傳說故事七個聚落之一。

巴拉冠（palakuwan）：在卑南語中，指的是成年男子聚會活動的場所，也有人稱「男人屋」，現在中文一般稱做「會所」。

神秘的月形石柱

一時之間，天搖地動，大火蔓燒，拉拉鄂斯人居住的
地方幾乎化為灰燼，只留下一座又一座神秘的大石
柱，筆直豎立在天地之間，彷彿向後人訴說著這一場
浩劫的故事。

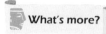

What's more?

拉拉鄂斯人：目前尚難明確指出拉拉鄂斯人是哪一族群的
人。

甘蔗：aspan，阿斯班。

臭鼬：kuyu，古由。

很久很久以前，卑南族有一對少年兄弟，哥哥奧那樣和弟弟依布萬，經常在夜裡，偷偷地潛入鄰近拉拉鄂斯人所種的甘蔗園中，去偷取汁液甜美的甘蔗。兩兄弟在偷的時候，口中常學臭鼬的聲音，發出「吱吱～～吱吱～～吱吱～～」的叫聲來欺騙拉拉鄂斯人。

不久，拉拉鄂斯人到甘蔗園察看，發現甘蔗不像是被臭鼬啃過的樣子，反倒像是有人進出的痕跡。於是，拉拉鄂斯人便用灰燼灑在甘蔗園四周。

隔天拉拉鄂斯人再去察看時，果然發現是人類的腳印，便確定有人偷採了他們的作物。

當晚，拉拉鄂斯人事先埋伏，不知情的兩兄弟仍假裝臭鼬的叫聲進入甘蔗園，拉拉鄂斯人一湧而上要捉拿他們。

奧那樣因為個子比較高，一跳就跳出甘蔗園的石砌圍牆。依布萬個子矮，沒有跳過去，被捉住了。拉拉鄂斯人便把依布萬關進會所，並派人看守著。

奧那樣逃走以後，十分擔心依布萬的安危，絞盡腦汁，終於想到了一個辦法。奧那樣以藤片做了一個很大的風箏，準備爬到卑南大溪對岸的富源山上去放。

援救計畫執行的前一天，奧那樣悄悄地潛入拉拉鄂斯人的會所邊，躲過守衛，隔著竹壁把計畫告訴依布萬，要他配合。

放風箏的那一天，依布萬在會所裡，聽到嗡嗡的聲響，知道奧那樣已經放出了風箏。嗡嗡聲也吸引了看管會所的拉拉鄂斯人，他們都很好奇的跑出

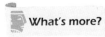

What's more?

風箏（tuwap，都瓦布）：以籐片編成兩個正方形再疊合成八角形，研究風箏的學者說，八角風箏是台灣傳統特有的形式。

來觀看這不曾見過的東西，議論紛紛，看得出神。

被關在會所裡的依布萬跟看守的人說：「是什麼東西在空中響呀？可不可以讓我靠近一點，到窗邊瞧一瞧。」看守人答應了他的請求。

依布萬到了窗邊之後，又說：「在窗邊看不清楚天上的風箏，可不可以讓我到門口來看一下？」看守人就讓他到門口來看風箏。

依布萬站在門口看了一會兒，又說：「在這裡還是太遠了，可不可以讓我到廣場中央去，和大家站在一塊兒看風箏，這樣才能看個清楚。」看守人心想在眾人的圍繞下依布萬肯定跑不掉，於是就同意讓他到廣場和大家一起看風箏。

夾雜在人群中看風箏的依布萬，又對看守人說：「我的個子太矮了，在廣場中和大家一起看，都被大家擋住了，還是看不清楚，可不可以讓我站到那個石臼上面看？」

依布萬又再次獲得允許，終於站到石臼上面看風箏。只見風箏忽上忽下的飄浮著，大家都看呆了。

依布萬又說：「真是稀奇的東西，借我一把刀，我可以把那天上飛的東西砍下來。」看守人不疑有他，而且也想看依布萬如何砍下風箏，所以就把刀借給了他。

遠在富源山上的奧那樣看到人群聚集，便駕御風箏上下俯衝，當風箏第三次往下衝時，依布萬拿了刀假裝要砍風箏，卻忽然躍起伸手拉住風箏的長尾巴，轉眼間，他的身子竟隨著風箏飛上天空。奧那樣見到依布萬已經抓住風箏了，立刻收線，風箏就高高地飛上天空了。

What's more?

石臼：在卑南遺址出土物中有石臼，但呈現缽形狀者為多。

到了天空，依布萬順手把借來的刀拋下，那刀正巧落在一位懷孕婦人的肚子上，將婦人的肚子從中剖開生出了雙胞胎。

眼見依布萬騰空離去，拉拉鄂斯人才恍然大悟，但是要追也來不及了，只能眼睜睜地看他逃離。

奧那樣把風箏拉往卑南大溪北邊的富源山頂。當依布萬落地後，奧那樣得知他被拉拉鄂斯人強逼吞食骯髒污穢又噁心的東西，又氣又憐，急忙叫依布萬把吃下的東西都吐出來。依布萬因而吐出所有的東西，它們竟然變成了水池。傳說中，卑南族人稱這個水池為卡那勒洌，池水永不乾涸，只是始終有股難聞的怪味。

由於依布萬遭到虐待，在他脫困以後，兩兄弟想要報仇雪恨，便去請教住在巴巴都蘭的外祖母姐達姥。

外祖母姐達姥說：「那就讓天降下黑暗給拉拉鄂斯人好了。」於是黑暗降下，世界一片漆黑。

但是拉拉鄂斯人在黑暗中，還是能以雙手觸摸東西，憑感覺將乾的木柴挑出來升火煮東西、取暖。黑暗對拉拉鄂斯人的生活並沒有造成太大的影響，反而使自己的族人也跟著不方便。

於是，奧那樣和依布萬又去問外祖母姐達姥說：「拉拉鄂斯人還是可以照常生活，反而是我們變得不方便！這樣不好，要怎麼樣才能再恢復白天的生活呢？」

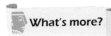

What's more?

雙胞胎：在卑南族人的傳統觀念中，生雙胞胎是不吉祥的。

卡那勒洌（kanaLeLya）：有嘔吐的意思。這個水池位在台東縣卑南鄉富源村內，不過因開路的緣故，池水已經填蓋枯竭了。

巴巴都蘭：位於現在的台東市卑南遺址的附近。

外祖母姐達姥說：「即然如此，你們就到都蘭山，向住在那裡的老人家借白色的雞，並且讓牠啼叫。等到牠第三次啼叫的時候，天就會亮了。」

奧那樣和依布萬照著外祖母姐達姥的話去做，天果然就亮了。天亮之後，兩兄弟還是覺得不服氣，又去問外祖母姐達姥其他可以消滅拉拉鄂斯人的辦法。

外祖母姐達姥聽了便說：「你們到天界去下地震吧！」

於是奧那樣和依布萬搬了很多的石頭，把外祖母姐達姥的房子四周給圍起來，讓房子更為堅固，又以扁石板圍住，並頂在房子四周。然後，把房子周圍的檳榔樹都綁上鐵片，再用繩子把所有的檳榔樹綁成一圈。

奧那樣和依布萬把這些安全措施完成後，告訴外祖母姐達姥說：「當您聽到第一聲雷響時，就知道我們兩個人已經到了天上。」

奧那樣和依布萬到了天界，催動雷聲和地震，地上也響起了鐵片聲。奧那樣和依布萬不斷聽鐵片聲調整震幅，希望不要波及外祖母姐達姥的房子。然後，奧那樣和依布萬才放手催動地震，讓大地搖個不停，火災不斷，四處蔓延燃燒。

過了許久，外祖母姐達姥覺得燒得差不多了，就跟兩兄弟說：「夠了啦，孩子啊，可以了啦，已經沒有拉拉鄂斯人了啊！好了，夠了！」

奧那樣和依布萬聽到了外祖母姐達姥的喊聲後，才把地震止住。只見拉拉鄂斯人居住的達拉拉不灣都已經化成灰燼，而那些沒有倒塌的屋壁，也都化為石頭，筆直地豎立在當地。

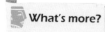 **What's more?**

雞：turukuk，都魯咕克。

如今留下的東西，就僅剩卑南遺址上的「月形石柱」而已，至於拉拉鄂斯人早已被毀滅了。

由於這個神話故事的關係，卑南族人一直把卑南遺址，也就是拉拉鄂斯人居住的達拉拉不灣，視為禁地。

Where did it come from?
本故事由台東市寶桑里的林仁誠先生講述，人類學家宋龍生採集，經作者刪修，再請陳光榮長老提供意見。

What's more?

達拉拉不灣（talalabuwan）：為「廢墟」的意思，所指的地方就是現在的卑南遺址，而這個地方卑南族人始終視為禁地，他們認為死過人的地方會有惡靈存在，告誡子孫不可靠近；同時也提醒後人悲劇不要重演。

月形石柱：卑南遺址地表上曾經留下了許多大型的石柱，而這些石柱大致確認是建築的一部分，不過使用的方式則尚在討論，目前新的推論認為很可能是立在房屋建築的中央部位，當中柱使用。

感恩海祭的由來

每年夏天小米收割之後，就到了卑南族南王部落的祭祀季節，族人帶著小米來到海邊，也來到卑南大溪北岸溪邊，虔誠祭獻。海祭在南王部落中一代傳過一代，感恩的心也跟著傳遞下來。

卑南族南王部落有一個特殊的感恩祭儀，叫海祭，是其他各部落所沒有的。這個祭儀通常在夏天小米收割以後舉行，成年的男子們會帶著小米到海邊，面向蘭嶼、面向綠島，還到卑南大溪北岸溪邊面對都蘭山，向祖先舉行感恩祭獻的儀式。

為什麼會在三個地點同時舉行祭獻儀式呢？因為感恩海祭是由三種不同的神話及傳說所構成的，所以到了該向祖先表達感謝的季節時，南王部落人會分別在三個不同的地點，同時舉行感恩的儀式。

感恩海祭由來之一

◆ 尋找小米種子

古早以前，一位南王部落的祖先叫德馬拉紹，為了尋找可以當做主食的植物，來到東方的海上。

有一天，他到了布肚兒島，並愛上了島上一位名字叫黛斑的美麗姑娘，黛斑也愛著這位由外地來的英俊青年，並表示願意嫁給他。

德馬拉紹和黛斑成家以後，並沒有忘記他最初的目的。德馬拉紹在布肚兒島上不斷地尋找，終於發現島上居民所食用的珍貴小米。於是，德馬拉紹和妻子黛斑便想將小米的種子攜回台灣部落，分享給族人。

但是，布肚兒島上的居民非常珍視小米這種植物，對它管制非常嚴格，不允許任何人將它帶離布肚兒島。

德馬拉紹和黛斑想盡了一切可行的藏匿方法，把種子藏在腋下，藏在頭髮，藏在眼皮，藏在耳朵，藏在嘴巴，藏在鼻孔，但是每一次都被發現，遭到沒收。

德馬拉紹和黛斑雖然屢試屢敗，但仍意志堅定鍥而不捨，最後，德馬拉紹想出了一個不得已的方法，他將小米的種子，藏到自己的私處，終於瞞過了島上的居民，成功地將妻子和小米的種子帶出布肚兒島，回到部落。

離開布肚兒島的時候，黛斑的哥哥巫馬魯道也隨他們一同前往，但是巫馬魯道住了一段時間以後，由於非常思念家鄉，決定回布肚兒島。

離別前夕，巫馬魯道請求妹夫和妹妹每年小米收割以後，要帶釀好的小米酒到海邊去，搭配當場煮好的小米粥，向布肚兒島獻祭。

 What's more?

布肚兒島：指台東外海的蘭嶼。

德馬拉紹和黛斑將這件事牢牢記在心裡，每年到了小米收割完成之後，一定依約到海邊舉行祭獻的儀式，表達感謝並祈禱來年豐收。

由於德馬拉紹和黛斑是南王部落沙巴樣氏族和拉拉氏族的祖先，所以向布肚兒島祭獻的人，主要以南王部落中沙巴樣氏族和拉拉氏族的後裔為主。

Where did it come from?

本故事由台東市南王社區發展協會理事長陳光榮長老講述。

What's more?

小米收割：每年到了七月中旬，小米成熟飽滿，這時正是收割小米最好的時機。

感恩海祭由來之二

◆ 向大魚報恩

從前南王部落的阿拉西斯氏族，有個名叫巴塔吉烏的祖先，是出了名的搗蛋鬼。巴塔吉烏很喜歡在族人舂米做糯米糕的時候惡作劇，他會故意在別處高喊失火求救的呼聲，引誘大家前去救火，自己卻趁機闖入族人的屋內偷取所有的糯米糕。

族人空跑幾次之後，發現是巴塔吉烏在惡作劇，紛紛向他的家人控訴。'

巴塔吉烏的行為惡劣行徑，讓家人傷透腦筋，深深感到羞恥；但家人屢次規勸，巴塔吉烏仍然不改他搗蛋的行為。巴塔吉烏的舅舅古拉流，特別和部落裡的人講好，打算把巴塔吉烏放逐到不能回到部落的地方。

有一天，古拉流和族中的男人們約巴塔吉烏一起到海上的小島沙那山打獵。傳說，沙那山就是現在的綠島。

那時，台灣島和沙那山島之間有一棵很大很長的榕樹根做為橋樑相連。一行人就利用榕樹根來到沙那山。

到了沙那山之後，古拉流指揮大家分散到原野各處，把野獸趕出來，並進行圍捕。活躍的巴塔吉烏興高彩烈地奔向原野深處去趕野獸，但是，他萬萬想不到，這竟是親人故意設下的計謀。

What's more?

舂米：卑南語中「杵」叫拉速克（rasuk），「臼」稱打畢（tabi），而舂小米或稻米的動作叫做馬地那班（maTinapan）。

沙那山：指台東外海的綠島。

當巴塔吉烏深入沙那山時，隨行的人立刻從原來的大榕樹根上撤回，並且將它切斷，令人討厭的巴塔吉烏便永遠無法再回到部落。

巴塔吉烏忙了一陣子之後，不見其他人的蹤影，來到大榕樹根旁邊，發現樹根已經被切斷，才知道自己被族人放逐了。巴塔吉烏望著茫茫的大海，只能徬徨無助的傷心哭泣。

然而，巴塔吉烏的哭聲讓天神起了憐憫之心。

天神知道巴塔吉烏徬徨無助，於是命令一隻大魚載他渡海回家。大魚告訴巴塔吉烏：「當我潛入海水時，如果你感覺呼吸困難，請捏我的魚鰓，我就會浮出海面換氣；如果到了岸邊，就捏三下。」

沈浮三次以後，來到靠近台東貓山的岸邊，大魚用牠的尾巴把巴塔吉烏拋上海灘，巴塔吉烏也因而獲救回到自己的部落。

上岸時，巴塔吉烏因腳站不穩而翻滾摔跤，從此以後巴塔吉烏得了一個新的名字，叫「阿里特阿里特」，也就是「摔跤」的意思。

巴塔吉烏上岸後，大魚在海中頻頻回頭交待說：「每年在小米收成之後，要按時到海邊來供奉我。」

從此以後，巴塔吉烏再也不搗蛋了，而且每年巴塔吉烏所屬的阿拉西斯氏族的所有成年男子，都要經過貓山到靠向沙那山的海邊，祭謝大魚的救命之恩。

感恩海祭由來之三

◆ 請山神吃新米

巴沙拉阿特氏族的祖先，有一天涉水過卑南大溪，到北岸耕作、砍材，中午吃飯的時候，發現掛在牛車上的飯簍裡，竟然有一條百步蛇。

他在驚慌中打翻了飯簍，心中一面有著不祥的感覺，又猛然想到，可能是因為再過幾天才要舉行海祭，而在海祭之前涉水過卑南大溪，對山神是不敬的，心想，應該趕快拿今年夏天收成的小米來祭拜謝罪，否則即使溪水很淺，也可能隨時會發生意外。

從此，巴沙拉阿特氏族以及和他們有關係的巴拉阿度氏族的後裔，每年在海祭當天都會特地涉過卑南大溪，到北岸舉行祭禮，向山神祈福謝罪。

Where did it come from?
本故事由台東市南王社區發展協會理事長陳光榮長老講述。

What's more?

百步蛇（maiDang，麥讓）：有長老的意思。

山神（myaibar，米愛拔兒）：山的掌控者。

部落百寶盒｜｜傳授哈「原」秘笈，搖身變成卑南通

一、普悠瑪的主要部落

卑南族是台灣原住民族群之一，分佈於花東縱谷尾端，台東扇狀平原附近，共有八個主要部落，因而昔日有「八社番」的稱呼。八社分別是：知本（katipul，台東市建業里）：射馬干（kasabakan，今稱建和部落，台東市建和里）；呂家（Likavung，今稱利嘉部落，卑南鄉利嘉村）；大巴六九（Tamalakaw，今稱泰安部落，卑南鄉泰安村）；阿里擺（alipay，今稱上賓朗部落，卑南鄉賓朗村之頂永豐）；北絲鬮（uLibuLibek，今稱初鹿部落，卑南鄉初鹿村）；卑南（puyuma，今稱南王部落，台東市南王里）；賓朗（pinasiki，今稱下賓朗部落，卑南鄉賓朗村之下賓朗）。

另外，還有寶桑（papuLu），在今台東市博愛里，是後來由卑南部落遷出的部分族人逐漸聚成的，而龍過脈（dandanaw）則是由初鹿部落分出的聚落。目前卑南族大約有一萬人之多。

根據人類學家宋龍生的研究，按起源傳說的不同，將卑南族八個部落分為兩大群落：

一為以知本為主的知本社群，含射馬干、呂家、大巴六九、阿里擺、北絲鬮等部落；他們一般相信「石生」的始祖創生神話，以「陸發岸」（ruhuahan）為發源地。

二為以卑南部落為主的南王社群，含南王、賓朗、寶桑等部落；他們一般相信「竹生」的始祖創生神話，以「把那巴那揚」（panapanayan）為發源地。此外，晚近有第三種起源傳說，就是本書收錄「都蘭山下的普悠瑪」的故事。

由於知本社群與排灣族、魯凱族毗鄰，語言及風俗文化等等，明顯受到兩族的影響；而南王社群因與海岸山脈兩麓人口眾多的阿美族相鄰，交互影響亦深。當然，由於卑南族地處台東沖積平原地帶，漢族的移入所帶動的農業發展，不但使卑南族較早脫離部落型的經濟型態，也使卑南族成為漢化較深的原住民族群。

普悠瑪部落（卑南部落），其實指的是現今南王部落，它原位在卑南平原（或稱台東平原）的北方，部落座落在卑南大溪沖積的廣闊河階上，部落的北方隔著卑南大溪且面向都蘭山，向東約五、六公里遠便臨太平洋，西方有卑南山（海拔不超過二百公尺的小丘），而部落的南方則是太平溪。這塊夾在卑南大溪及太平溪間的樂土，南北寬約三、四公里，東西長約六、七公里的範圍內，是傳統卑南族人居住、耕作的家園。

小米曾經是部落最重要的主糧，不過到了清代乾隆年間，距今約二百多年前，部落中的拉拉（ra'ra）氏族有位叫比那來（pinaDay）的人，因緣際會，曾經到屏東枋寮、水底寮一帶生活，向漢人學到了種植水稻的方法後，將水稻耕作的方式引進部落，使卑南族人的農業生產得到改善，並進而提升到政治軍事的影響力，他更因協助清朝平亂有功，被清朝封為六品官。

不過，民間卻傳說比那來被清朝封為「卑南王」，勢力最盛的時候，統轄的領域北達花蓮瑞穗鄉，南抵屏東恒春一帶，成為七十二個部落的盟主。到了日本時期，日本人看中了這一片沃野，積極推展蔗糖事業，卑南族人又接觸到了新的經濟性作物；現在，這裡的農民，又有了最新的興趣，那就是栽種味甜而美的高經濟作物——釋迦。

▶ 都蘭山下的普悠瑪

1	都蘭山	卑南族南王部落人心中的聖山。
2	阿邦安	卑南族祖先遷移時，老人留居的地方。
3	卑南大溪	
4	拉拉鄂斯人的聚落	傳說被卑南族人以巫術摧毀，因而成為後來的卑南遺址。
5	昔日的普悠瑪部落	雖然從部落距離太平洋很近，但卑南族人並不靠海討生活。

6	虎頭山	
7	石頭山	
8	馬高瓦高山、馬里瓦色得山	依布萬乘風降落時，雙腳著地時推出的兩座小山。
9	卡那得冽池	依布萬被拉拉鄂斯人強吞骯髒的東西，而嘔吐物成了水池。

二、「會所制度」知多少？

相對於人口眾多的阿美族、排灣族，人口稀少的卑南族之所以能輾轉其間而獨立自存，實賴於其傳統文化、社會中一些特質，其中最重要的便是卑南族嚴格斯巴達式的「會所制度」（palakuwan）。

按卑南族的習慣，男子十二、三歲以後，即進入「會所」，並終其一生屬於會所的成員。會所分為兩個大的組織：首先是「少年會所」（TakuTakuban），成員是卑南族十二、十三歲至十六、十七歲的青少年。他們按年齡形成一個嚴格的年齡階層，經過五至六年的考驗與訓練，成為「米亞布丹」（miyaputan），準備晉級至「邦沙浪」（bangsaran）階段。這段時期的養成過程是極為嚴酷的，青少年們在一級管一級以及長輩們指導、要求之下，不但要學習各種內在精神和意志的鍛練，例如禮節、服從、膽識、謙卑、忍耐等等，同時也要增強體能，學習各種狩獵、耕作、建築等生活技藝，更重要的是要學習各項戰鬥技術，使他們成為社會、經濟、軍事與文化的中堅。「少年會所」因而成為卑南族男子社會化最重要的機制，也是凝聚族群力量的強固基礎。

在每年一度年底「猴祭」（mangayangayaw）和「大獵祭」（mangayaw）祭儀活動之後，「少年會所」的老大哥「米亞布丹」便晉級為「邦沙浪」，進入所謂的「成人會所」。在這個階段，卑南族青年雖不像少年會所那樣要受到各種各樣的訓練，但他們仍受上一年齡階層長輩的節制。他們可以說是卑南族社會活動的主體，是第一線的服役成員。他們一方面要秉承老年、壯年長輩的指導，實際負起部落各項的責任；另一方面也負責少年會所的訓練和監督。一般認為「會所制度」是卑南族之所以能成功地周旋於各大族間的利器。

傳統卑南族是母系社會，財產的承繼由母傳長女，在婚姻形態上採行招贅方式。但由於「會所制度」的存在，使卑南族社會在男女角色上有明確的分工。男子透過「會所」成為部落政治權力的主體，對部落的公共事務握有絕對的支配、決定力；而女子在財產和家族性事務上，擁有相當的發言甚至決定權。

卑南族人每年在十月份，集合部落中的少年人合力搭蓋「少年會所」，猴祭結束便毀棄，待明年再建。而「成人會所」則始終保留完好，族中未結婚的成年男子，時常都在此聚集、守護。

當然，因時代變遷，傳統習慣也有了一些改變。

▶ 少年會所的平面圖解

火爐：晚上少年們團聚在爐火前烤火，聆聽高年級少年的訓示。

床和座位：座位依照年齡大小，分別由入口處開始往逆時鐘方向安排，少年會所內由高年級管低年級。

▶ 少年會所的立體圖解

1	置物間 或置猴處	平時存放物品；也是猴祭祭儀進行中，暫放猴屍的地方。
2	竹梯子	架起竹梯子，方便進入會所內。
3	屋頂	
4	陽台	平時的用途為瞭望遠處動靜，在猴祭結束時，少年會站在上面將象徵幸運物的物件（現在多為木雕刻的棒子和糖果）往下丟擲，族人會在下面爭相撿拾，希望帶來好運。

5	斜柱	用粗大的竹子排列架成,稱為「干欄式建築」。
6	直立柱	
7	墊腳石	又稱護神石,為少年和外界(包括女性)接觸的界限。
8	角力	戰鬥訓練之一,目的在訓練少年高昂的鬥志,並由少年們相互扭打纏鬥的動作中,隱喻明年穀物結實纍纍。
9	打屁股	在少年期,多半性情浮躁,行事較為莽撞,高年級者執藤條體罰,主要是提醒少年做事小心,期望他們能做個思慮周密的大人。

三、年祭巡禮：猴祭

年祭是卑南族年度最重要的祭儀，通常在年底舉行，現在大約固定在每年十二月二十日至隔年的一月三日間舉行。整個祭儀，主要分為兩大部分：一是「猴祭」，以少年會所為主體；另一是「大獵祭」，以成人會所為主體。接下來，我們依南王部落的習俗，做扼要介紹。

關於猴祭祭儀的過程，大致如下：

▶ 修葺會所（puba'aw）

這個儀式過去是在六月底七月初稻子收割之後，配合會所開訓舉行，在級生和新入的少年們會回到會所生活。不過進入會所之前，先要由祭師行竹占問卜擇日，並進行會所建築物材料的換新和維修。現在由於會所功能被學校取代，會所維修的時間就移到十二月二十日左右，在大獵祭開始前，各家總動員一起維修。

▶ 祭告祖靈（temuliyabak）

第二天由祭師帶領少年組最高年級的成員祭拜神明及祖靈。之後，由少年領導進行用糯米糕問卜的儀式，如果丟上會所平台呈半弧形糯米糕的面朝上，顯示獵猴順利；反之，就必須加倍努力。

▶ 禳災祈福（semilap）

第三天祭師們在部落的四個角落設祭壇，並輪流祭禱祖靈（含當年往生者）、驅除邪靈、祈求神明降福、賜予平安。

▶ 設立守護門（semaLikiD）

第四天取長竹子及長野藤，在部落四處入口設立拱門，再由祭師們祭禱，以阻止邪靈進入部落。

▶ 整修祭壇（merawak）

第五天到野外預定地清除雜草，設立刺猴祭壇，並將所獵到的猴移進祭壇中的柵欄裡。入夜，少年們進行膽識訓練（parlimalimaw）。

▶ 新米啟用祭（gemamuL）

第六天由各家族長老帶領族人，各抓一把當年收割的新米，到村外的新米祭壇，向北方的都蘭山行撒米儀式，請祖先降靈啟用新米，之後才可以食用新米。

入夜之後，少年會所中的高年級領導們，會帶領低年級者各持乾香蕉葉，挨家挨戶行熱鬧的少年驅邪儀式（semimusimuk又稱halabakay）。驅邪儀式結束後的深夜，在部落長老的監督下，南北兩少年會所的成員，會在部落外的休耕地上，進行激烈的群體角力賽（mapingipingiT），其目的在訓練高昂的鬥志，並由少年們相互扭纏的動作中，象徵明年穀物結實纍纍。

▶ 猴祭

行祭當日，所有少年各依級等盛裝參加祭儀，由早到午後，少年們依序要進行：為喪家除喪、刺猴、悼亡猴、棄猴、除舊佈新、擲糖祈福、享用美食，以及歌舞歡慶等儀禮活動。古時，在猴祭完成後，少年們會將刺死的猴子屍體丟到成年男子會所前，敦促大人儘速出獵。

四、年祭巡禮：大獵祭

猴祭結束後，隨即舉行大獵祭，這是成人出獵的活動，也是整個祭儀的高潮，成年男子從部落出發開始；儀式活動約略可以劃分為出發、行獵和凱歸慶祝等三大階段。

▶ 第一個階段：出發儀式

出發之前必做的一件事情，就是祭師們會在出發前，先到野外進行鳥占（kiayaayam），以占鳥的叫聲，決定出獵的方向與吉凶。在男子出獵前夕，婦女們會準備菸酒、糕點和禦寒衣物做為禮物，送給即將出獵的親人，使彼此之間的關係更加緊密，這樣的行為稱為布打甫（putabu）。

出發日的早晨，男子集合後出發，正受成年訓練的米亞布丹們，要背負自己族父的行李上路。「族父」，其實就是引領米亞布丹進入成年的引導者，卑南語叫布發里森（pubaLisen），通常是由米亞布丹的父母選擇部落內足當楷模的長輩來擔任，他成了米亞布丹部落的父親，扮演真正教養的工作，其重要性有時候比自己親生的父母還大。

當隊伍到了離開部落不遠的路途時，祭師們會以甜根子草（禾本科甘蔗屬，葉寬約一公分，但比五節芒窄，夏天開花。）橫置於路上，佈置象徵劃分聖界與凡界的門檻，再以去蒂的檳榔為祭禮，阻謝該年過世的族人亡靈跟隨，所有參獵的族人都要跨越，以避邪求平安。

到了獵場，在祭師舉行祭山儀式（purinakep）後，眾人隨即分工合作，搭建營地。營地照例分做兩處，其中一處是為當年喪家親人所住，不能混居。除非經過除喪的儀式，喪家是不潔淨的。

▶ 第二個階段：行獵

行獵間，不同的年齡階級各有職司，米亞布丹負責雜務及侍奉長老，青壯年負責行獵和營地安全；而長老則是留營壓陣，閒暇時製作各種器具以贈送族人，並指導米亞布丹各種生活的技能。

夜晚是大家圍火共聚的時刻，長老們會以吟唱（pairairaw）的方式，傳頌祖先事蹟。不過，此舉也可能引來敵人的窺伺和攻擊，所以青壯年們會領著米亞布丹，徹夜呼喊巡繞營地，警告暗處的敵人，不要輕舉妄動，並不斷地把芒草莖製成的箭矢射向營外黑暗處，逼使隱匿的敵人現出蹤跡。

▶ 第三個階段：凱歸

打獵完畢驗收成果之後，即拔營回部落，而部落婦女們為迎接男子們的凱歸，會預先在部落之外，以竹子搭建迎獵門（muLaLipad）。當日婦女們都會帶著自家男子的禮服、花環和佳餚美酒，穿著盛裝在迎獵門處，等候歸來的男子們。男子們抵達後，便由婦女們為他們更換禮服，戴上一串又一串的花環，然後與家人歡聚吟唱，更會為喪家舉行除喪之禮。

迎禮結束，青壯年們圍繞著長老，浩浩蕩蕩地返回部落的會所廣場。在會所裡，一方面由族父為當年已屆成年的米亞布丹換裝戴冠，一方面引領喪家親人走入廣場中共舞，藉此表示完成除喪。入夜後，新晉級成年者會在歌舞聲中被引介，往往通宵達旦。次日長老們會到每戶喪家吟唱「解憂」，鼓勵他們迎接新生活。之後，部落一連歡慶歌舞數日，大獵祭才算告一段落。

五、卑南遺址

卑南遺址位於火車站台東新站的後方，遺址廣約一百公頃，是以台灣新石器時代晚期（約三千五百年前至二千年前）存在東台灣地區史前卑南文化系列中，最大最重要的遺址。

卑南遺址堆疊存在著兩個不同時期的文化，低層較古老的文化是屬於台灣新石器時代中期的東部繩紋紅陶文化（約四千五百年前到三千五百年前），上層較晚近的文化是台灣新石器時代晚期的史前卑南文化（約三千五百年前至二千年前）。

時間	重要事件
1896年	日本學者鳥居龍藏是最早到卑南遺址的學者，留下了兩張卑南遺址板岩石柱的照片。
1920年	日本學者鹿野忠雄詳細記錄石柱的特色、大小、排列情形，並提及卑南族的傳說，並推測這裏曾有一「番社集團」。
1945年	日本學者金關丈夫及國分直一兩位考古學者曾進行約三週的小規模試掘工作，並將此地訂名為「卑南遺址」。
1945年後	有許多中外學者不斷前來，但是都未進行正式的發掘。
1980年夏	興建台東新站及其他相關工程時，工程單位在遺址的精華區挖出大量的石板棺及其他史前遺物。
1980年9月至1988年	台大人類學系宋文薰及連照美兩位教授為了搶救古物，在文建會及台東縣政府的委託下，共進行了十三次的發掘工作，使遺址聲名大噪。
1988年	由於卑南遺址可以說是台灣考古學史上發掘面積最大的遺址，為進一步保護國家重要文化資產，由內政部評定為一級古蹟。
1990年2月	經地方人士及學者們的構思與奔走，「國立台灣史前文化博物館籌備處」正式成立，並設立「卑南文化公園」。
2001年7月	「國立台灣史前文化博物館」正式成立。

卑南遺址出土物中，最令人印象深刻的是密集的墓葬（石板棺群）及其精美的陪葬品，其次則是宏偉的建築遺跡（石柱）。目前已出土的石板棺數量超過一千六百座以上，且都成南北同一個方向整齊排列。而陪葬品方面，有各式精美的玉器、磨製石器和各式完整的陶罐，包括玉製或蛇紋岩製的錛（木工用具）、鑿（鑽器）、矛鏃（武器）、管珠（胸飾）、玉棒（飾品）、玦（耳飾）、手環、玉鈴（飾品）等。除此之外，還有石牆結構、人骨及獸骨等，為我們留下了解讀台灣古代生活的豐富訊息。有機會，不訪親身造訪卑南遺址。

六、海祭之歌

海祭是在夏季舉行的祭儀，一定要在小米成熟收成後舉行，以陽曆而言，約在七月中旬左右，實際的日子由部落長老們共同選擇決定。

海祭當天一大早，首先由祭司分別到拉拉（ra'ra）、巴沙拉阿特（pas-ara'aT）、阿拉西斯（arasis）三氏族的祖靈屋中行祭，祭後分別到往蘭嶼、往綠島的海邊，以及卑南大溪的北岸，各家後裔的男性依其所屬，參加海邊的祭儀。

在海邊的祭場，會搭建讓祖靈來休息的小棚和獻祭物品用的置物架；而在卑南大溪北岸的祭場，則只做掛小米飯的掛架。祭物是酒、檳榔和小米飯，小米飯要在祭場烹煮獻祭，而在獻祭時，每人以手沾小米飯和酒撒向祖先的方向。

過去，往來祭場都是用走路的，現在在祭畢後（約近中午時分），男子們先搭車至部落附近，便下車依古禮跑步回會所廣場，各家婦女都會在廣場準備食物等候。男子們一到，即開席使用中餐，現在中餐時順便會安排母語演唱比賽之類的活動。下午，進行全部落男子（從幼稚園男童到成年）的摔角比賽，有時候晚間也會安排遊藝晚會活動，全村一同來歡樂，金曲歌王陳建年及紀曉君等人出名前也都曾登台表演過！

由於對海祭獨特的情懷，南王部落都曾流傳過和它相關的歌曲，而其中最著名的一首〈海祭〉即是由卑南族音樂家陸森寶先生所作。陸森寶曾經是運動健將，在日據時期得過全台四百及八百公尺冠軍，因而保送台南師範學校。到了台南才接觸到鋼琴，因為興趣加上天份，很快就學會了彈奏的技巧，並在日本皇太子到訪問時，奉命演奏。

陸森寶所創作的歌曲大都是以南王部落的風景以及民情風俗為主題的歌曲，他愛鄉的情懷都在他的作品表現出來，例如〈美麗的稻穗〉、〈蘭嶼頌〉等等。晚近成名的「金曲歌王」陳建年（本書繪圖者），就是陸森寶的外孫，他繼承了祖父的才華，更發揚光大。

造訪部落　　# 部落藏寶圖，來挖卑南寶

看過了卑南族的神話與傳說故事，和南王人一起仰望「聖山（都蘭山）」，親探神秘禁地「月形石柱（卑南遺址）」，感受南王部落對得來不易小米的海祭儀式，覺得意猶未盡吧！

卑南族主要有八個部落，分佈在台東市及台東縣卑南鄉，目前大約有一萬多人，過去有「八社番」的稱呼。但是，後來又遷移延伸出龍過脈和寶桑部落。現在，透過這份精心編製的「台東卑南族文化導覽圖」，邀請你盡情挖掘部落文化寶藏，保證不虛此行。

當然，造訪部落時更不能錯過卑南族豐富的祭儀活動，像是十二月底至一月初的「猴祭」和「大獵祭」、七月份的「收獲祭」及南王部落的「海祭」；至於卑南族在一九八九年新創的聯合年祭，從二　二年開始，決議每兩年舉辦一次，由各部落輪流主辦。心動想要行動之前，最好先確定時間及地點。

詳情請洽：

台東市所：電話：089-325301 網址http://www.taitungcity.gov.tw/

台東縣政府：電話：089-326141 網址http://www.taitung.gov.tw/

台東縣卑南鄉公所：電話：089-381368

卑南族
文化導覽圖

族語開口說　入境隨俗的卑南語

早安！
sinabalan!
西那巴蘭

晚安！
marawban!
馬勞班

你好嗎？
inaba　yu Dya?
依那巴　優　嗲
好　你　嗎

你精神好嗎？
saLiksik　yu Dya?
沙利克夕克　優　嗲
精神　　　你　嗎

我從南王部落來。
kemay ku　i puyuma.
哥麥　故　依　普悠瑪
從　普悠瑪 來（我）

我很高興遇見你。
semanagar ku　menau kanu.
斯馬嗯啊了　故　麼那勿　卡奴
高興　　　（我）見到　你

我的名字是阿吉拉賽。
nanku ngaLat　i agilasay.
南故　嗯阿拉特 依 阿吉拉賽
我的 名字　　是 阿吉拉賽

（請問）會所在那裡？
na paLakuwan i ulaya　isuwa?
那 巴拉冠　　依 烏拉亞 依蘇哇
那 會所　　　有 （是）在那裡

我想去會所
maranger ku　muka　i　palakuwan.
馬拉嗯了 故　母卡　依　巴拉冠
想　　　（我）去 （那）會所

你在做什麼？
kemakuda yu?
哥馬古打　優
做什麼　你

這是什麼？
amanay Dini(Di)?
阿馬奈　笛你（笛）
什麼　這個

那是什麼？
amanay Du?
阿馬奈　入
什麼　那個

我們在等待海祭的日子。
mengangara mi　kana　mulaliyaban tu wari
麼拉拉嗯阿　密　卡那　母拉里亞班　度 哇利
等待　　　我們 那個 海祭　　　的 日子

你歌唱得真好！
salaw bulay nu　　sinayan!
沙勞　不賴　奴　　西那樣
非常　美　你的　歌

你舞跳得真好！
salaw bulay nu niwarakan!
沙勞　不賴　奴　你哇拉幹
非常　好　你　跳舞

謝謝！
semangalan!
斯馬嗯阿蘭
謝謝（高興）

再見！（期待再相會！）
marepanauwa ta Dya!
馬了把那嗚哇　打嗲
再相見

我想念你。
masepeng ku　　kanu.
馬思奔　　故　　卡奴
想念　（我）　你

你好美！
salaw yu bulay!
沙勞　優 不賴
非常　你 美

你好帥！
salaw yu bangsar!
沙勞　優　棒沙了
非常　你　帥

你好酷（強）！
salaw yu makeser!
沙勞　優　馬克思了
非常　你　酷（強）

族語開口說　**卑南族稱謂的介紹**

ama	阿媽	爸爸、伯伯、叔叔、舅舅
mumu	姆姆	阿公或阿媽
ina	依那	媽媽、阿姨和姑姑

感謝：台東師院附屬實驗小學鄉土教育 林志美老師【阿萊黛（araytay）】校閱

學習加油站　**本書漢語與卑南語名詞對照表**

故事導讀：Puyuma，團結的花環

用漢字拼讀	卑南語	漢語名詞
姆勒哥撒達	murekesa ta	讓我們團結起來吧！

故事01：都蘭山下的普悠瑪

用漢字拼讀	卑南語	漢語名詞
都阿蘭（麥達安）	Tuangala（maiDangan）	都蘭山
沙古邦	sakuban	指今南王部落
普悠瑪	puyuma	卑南族族名；南王部落；團結
阿都如冒	adulumaw	男祖先名
阿都如紹	adulusaw	女祖先名
塔勒布	taLeb	舟筏
布肚兒	buTul	蘭嶼
麥達達兒	mayDadar	卑南族神話與傳說故事七聚落之一
巴巴都蘭	babaTulan	卑南族神話與傳說故事七聚落之一
阿拉阿拉外	arawaraway	卑南族神話與傳說故事七聚落之一
咕魯咕魯安	kulukulungan	卑南族神話與傳說故事七聚落之一
卡那巫肚	kanautu	卑南族神話與傳說故事七聚落之一
母奴奴弄	munununng	卑南族神話與傳說故事七聚落之一
布吉特	bukit	卑南族神話與傳說故事七聚落之一
阿邦安	apangan	當初老人休息之地
馬阿耀	mangayaw	大獵祭
格馬幕爾	gemamul	撒米祭獻儀式
巴拉冠	palakuwan	會所

故事02：神秘的月形石柱

用漢字拼讀	卑南語	漢語名詞
奧那樣	aunayan	人名
依布萬	ibuwan	人名
拉拉鄂斯人	raranges	族名
阿斯班	aspan	甘蔗
古由	kuyu	臭鼬
都瓦布	tuwap	風箏
卡覓 達 俄奈	kami Da enay	卑南大溪
打畢	tabi	石臼
馬阿阿比	maaapi	雙胞胎
卡那勒冽	kanaLeLya	地名
巴巴都蘭	babaTulan	地名
姐達姥	taDanaw	人名
都魯咕克	turukuk	雞
歌嗚金	geminggin	地震
不爛	pulan	檳榔樹
達拉拉布灣	talalabuwan	地名

故事03：感恩海祭的由來 / 由來之一：尋找小米種子

用漢字拼讀	卑南語	漢語名詞
幕拉里亞班	mulaliyaban	海祭
沙那山	sanasan	綠島
德馬拉紹	demaLasaw	祖先名
黛斑	tayban	女子名
達哇	dawa	小米
比尼	bini	種子
基度基度望	kiDukiDuwan	腋下
阿勒布	arebu	頭髮

用漢字拼讀	卑南語	漢語名詞
阿那努布	ananup	眼皮
答你拉	Tangila	耳朵
印單	indan	嘴巴
丁俄蘭	Tingelan	鼻孔
巫馬魯道	umaluDaw	男子名
布馬肚魯	pumadelu	獻祭
沙巴樣	sapayan	氏族名
拉拉	ra'ra'	氏族名

故事03：感恩海祭的由來 / 由來之二：向大魚報恩

用漢字拼讀	卑南語	漢語名詞
阿拉西斯	arasis	氏族名
巴塔吉烏	patakiu	男子名
拉速克	rasuk	杵
打畢	tabi	臼
馬地那班	maTinapan	椿米
古拉流	kuLaLui	人名
布吉特	bukit	貓山
阿里特阿里特	aliTaliT	摔跤

故事03：感恩海祭的由來 / 由來之三：請山神吃新米

用漢字拼讀	卑南語	漢語名詞
巴沙拉阿特	pasara'aT	氏族名
卡基巴	kakipa	牛車
麥讓	maiDang	百步蛇
米愛拔兒	myaibar	山神
巴拉阿度	balangatu	氏族名

部落百寶盒：普悠瑪部落

用漢字拼讀	卑南語	漢語名詞
卡地布	katipul	知本部落
卡沙發幹	kasabakan	建和部落，舊稱射馬干
利卡風	Likavung	利嘉部落，舊稱呂家
達瑪拉告	Tamalakaw	泰安部落，舊稱大巴六九
阿里擺	alipay	上賓朗部落，舊稱阿里擺
無理不理布克	uLibuLibek	初鹿部落，舊稱北絲鬮
普悠瑪	puyuma	南王部落，舊稱卑南
比那思齊	pinaski	下賓朗部落
巴布魯	papuLu	寶桑部落
坦達鬧	dandanaw	龍過脈部落
陸發岸	ruhuahan	石生系統發源地
把那巴那揚	panapanayan	竹生系統發源地
比那來	pinaDay	人名，人稱卑南王
馬高瓦高	magawwagaw	山名
馬里瓦色得	maliwaset	山名

部落百寶盒：「會所制度」知多少？

用漢字拼讀	卑南語	漢語名詞
巴拉冠	palakuwan	會所制度
打骨拔骨班	TakuTakuban	少年會所
米亞布丹	miyaputan	青少年期
邦沙浪	bangsaran	青少期
沙屋布	sa'up	屋頂
打卡兒	takar	陽台
沙勞沙勞灣	salawsalawwan	置物間或置猴處
拉里半	raripan	梯子
拉了得安	raredean	墊腳石

用漢字拼讀	卑南語	漢語名詞
把努把用	panubayun	斜柱
杜拉克	Turak	直立柱
馬阿亞阿耀	mangayangayaw	猴祭
馬阿耀	mangayaw	大獵祭

部落百寶盒：年祭巡禮：猴祭

用漢字拼讀	卑南語	漢語名詞
補拔奧	puba'aw	修葺會所
得母利亞巴克	temuliyabak	祭告祖靈
斯米拉布	semilap	禳災祈福
斯馬利基得	semaLikiD	設立守護門
母拉瓦克	merawak	整修祭壇
巴勒利馬利毛	parlimalimaw	膽識訓練
戈麻木兒	gemamuL	新米啟用祭
斯米母西母克（哈拉巴蓋）	semimusimuk（halabakay）	少年驅邪儀式
馬比你比你特	mapingipingiT	群體角力賽

部落百寶盒：年祭巡禮：大獵祭

用漢字拼讀	卑南語	漢語名詞
基阿亞阿雅母	kiayaayam	鳥占
布打甫	putabu	為打獵遠行者準備行李
布發里森	pubaLisen	族父
布里那哥布	purinakep	祭山儀式
巴依勞	pairairaw	吟唱
母拉里巴特	muLaLipad	迎獵門

造訪部落

卑南語用漢字拼讀	卑南語	漢語名詞
巴厄拉邦	Pa'labang	孫大川：本書總策劃
卡魯瑪安	Karuma'an	祖靈屋
包杜爾	pau-dull	陳建年：知名歌手
沙密娜特	samingad	紀曉君：知名歌手

卑南族南王部落 語音符號對照表

▶輔音

發音部位及方式	字母
雙唇塞音（清）	p
雙唇塞音（濁）	b
舌尖塞音（清）	t
舌尖塞音（濁）	d
舌根塞音（清）	k
舌根塞音（濁）	g
捲舌塞音（清）	T
捲舌塞音（濁）	D
舌尖擦音	s
雙唇鼻音	m
舌尖鼻音	n
舌根鼻音	ng
舌尖邊擦音	l
捲舌閃音	L
舌尖顫音	r
雙唇半元音	w
捲舌半元音	y

▶元音

發音部位	字母
高前元音	i
央元音	e
低央元音	a
高後元音	u

備註：「卑南族南王部落語音符號對照表」提供有興趣者，進一步學習卑南語者參考。

達悟族
Tao

- 達悟Tao語意是「人」，現在蘭嶼人都以達悟族自稱。
- 「雅美」一詞是日本人統治時所使用，也是現在台灣官方的稱法。
- 達悟的拼板舟、半穴居、語言、文化等，與菲律賓巴丹島相近，同為人類學家所稱的「南島語族」。

- 製造拼板舟大致有七種木材：龍骨與舟底可選用堅硬厚實的番龍眼、欖仁舅或蘭嶼赤楠，船身則選可浮在水面的輕質綠島榕、大葉山欖或麵包樹；並以小葉桑削成接合用的小木釘。
- 達悟人生性和平，不使用武器攻擊敵人、不獵首，近年來曾為核廢料問題憤怒抗爭。
- 每年3-6月是蘭嶼飛魚祭，但由於各地的大量捕捉，能夠隨著黑潮洄游到蘭嶼的飛魚已年年減少。

故事導讀　　大海的邏輯

古怪的人搭U字形的船來到蘭嶼，他們特異的能力似乎破壞了所有的常規，連花草樹木都不再茂盛，鳥兒也失去了往日的喜樂。就像其他世界地區共同流傳的神話母題一樣，一場大洪水淹沒了一切，大地用自己的力量淨化自己。

之後，島嶼恢復了生機，天上的人便降下祂自己的兩個孩子，一個在漁人部落為石生人，另一個在紅頭部落為竹生人。當他們各自生下一男一女之後，便喪失一切神力，成為完完全全的凡人。可見人雖然有神性的源頭，但他們不能再像古怪的人一樣，以其神力破壞常規；既然是人，就應當有人之道。竹生人和石生人決定將雙方的兒女相互嫁娶，避免近親繁衍，這是人倫綱紀的初始。之後，種種的價值規範便一一地被建立起來了。

對蘭嶼的達悟族人來說，他們最重要的倫理秩序，事實上大都來自於大海的啟示。飛魚是大海邏輯的使者，牠教導達悟族人如何分類？如何祭祀？如何生活？如何與人相處？又如何與大自然互動？說達悟族人的倫理是飛魚的倫理，是一種典型的海洋文明，應當不會是太過份的評斷。掌握了海的律動，達悟族人的心靈法則，便雖不中亦不遠矣。

既然成了凡人，我們便不能像怪人希・烏拉曼一樣，既能活在陸地上也能活在海裡面。達悟族人和海洋的關係，其接觸點就建立在他們一套複雜的拼板舟文化上。小船、大船的製造，從植樹、砍伐、拼製、完工到下水，每一個步驟都充滿禁忌和儀式，我們認為這是蘭嶼文化最核心的部分。而這套拼板舟製作技術的獲得，達悟族人謙虛地將功勞推給地底人。地底人的化身——老鼠，受命於天上的人，帶領十二名達悟族人，沿著水洞到他們地底下的家鄉，學習造船的技術。達悟族人後來發現，地底人的造船技術之所以那麼精良，不完全是純技術上的問題。根據地底人的教導，造船是一件非常莊嚴又神聖的事，需要男女分工合作，也需要學習尊重大自然，並且要遵守各式各樣的禁忌。這樣看起來，造舟其實就是倫理的實踐。

最後一則故事〈林投樹下的男孩〉，不僅反映了達悟族人對貞潔的看法，也讓我們看到那聰明、善良的男孩，如何公正地處理對自己養父母和對親生母親的孝道；他不但知恩圖報，又化解了對親生母親的恨意，那是正直、寬厚、健康的人格表現。

Logic of the Sea

The weird people took a U-shaped canoe to Orchid Island. Their peculiar abilities seemed to wreak chaos on and destroy all the routines and regimes of nature. Flowers and trees no longer flourished, and the birds lost their joy. As with mythological motifs shared by other parts of the world, a great flood submerged everything, with the earth using its intrinsic power to purify itself.

As the island regained its vitality, the people of the heavenly realm sent down two of their children: one born of the stone man in the fisher village, and the other born of the bamboo in the red head village. When the stone man and bamboo man had each given birth to a boy and a girl, they lost all their supernatural powers and became completely mortal. Although some people may possess the source of divinity, they can nevertheless not break the divine routine as did the weird people; they are human and they will have a human way. The man of bamboo and the man of stone decided their children would marry to avoid the issues from reproduction by close relatives. This was the beginning of human ethics following which various value norms were established one by one.

For the Tao people of Orchid Island, most of their important ethics order derives from the enlightenment of the sea. The flying fish conveys messages and logic of the sea. It teaches the Tao people classification, ritual, living, how to get along with people and how to get along with the rest of nature? To say that the ethics of the Tao are the ethics of the flying fish, or are ethics typical of an ocean based civilization, is actually right on point. The Tao, having mastered the rhythms of the sea, are never far from that which constitutes spiritual truth.

The point of contact between the Tao people and the ocean was based upon their complex canoe culture. The manufacturing of small and large canoes, from the planting of the trees whose wood will be used, felling those trees, assembling the various parts that have been carefully crafted as components of the canoe, completion of the vessel, and the elaborate ritual surrounding the vessel's maiden voyage, are all full of various taboo and ritual. This is the core of the Tao culture. Yet, the Tao people credit this set of complex skills to the people of the underground. A rat, sent by the heavens to the Tao, took twelve people through the water caves to the rat's underground home to teach the Tao the art of canoe construction. They learned that the canoe building process is a solemn and sacred undertaking, it requires the division of labor between men and women, learning to respect nature, and observing various taboos. Building of the canoe is the practice of an esthetic.

01

竹生人和石生人

> 一群長相古怪且行為怪異的人，四處撒野；不久之後，一場大洪水淹沒蘭嶼和這群人。

> 九年之後，春回大地，天上的人派祂的孩子——竹生人和石生人，延續達悟族人命脈，帶來智慧、知識，傳授技藝，並諄諄告誡後代族人要敬天惜物。

浩瀚的太平洋上，有一座非常神秘的島嶼，環海的四周有許多魚類和漂亮
貝殼。島上的樹木高大又茂盛，到處可以看到美麗的蘭花、百合花和山菊
花等等，還有五彩的珠光鳳蝶和可愛的白鼻心，以及夜間動物角鴞。

有一天，奇怪的事情發生了，海面上出現了一艘非常古怪的船，兩端尖尖
的，船身呈U字形，緩緩的駛近這座神秘的小島。

當船抵達小島時，一群長相古怪的人從船上走了下來，他們看起來非人、
非神、非鬼，有的肩膀非常寬大壯碩，有的眼睛特別大又凸出，有的手掌
很巨大但腳卻十分小。這群奇奇怪怪的人被這座景色優美的島嶼所吸引，
決定留下來居住。

他們的生活方式跟常人不一樣，每一個人都有特殊能力。

有一位名叫希‧巴雷的人，每次因為意見不和就會跟別人起衝突，常常被
打得不成模樣，卻有死而復生的能力，並且在海中和陸地上都一樣能夠生
活。

另外，有一位名叫希‧烏拉曼的人，他可以不必耕種，也不必到海邊捕
魚，好像不用吃任何東西就可以過活。

 What's more?

島嶼（pongso，碰樹）：故事中這座島嶼便是位在台東外海的蘭嶼，由於島
上西北角的岩石，在夕陽映照下，酷似印地安人的紅頭，因此舊稱「紅頭
嶼」。1946年，政府因該島盛產蝴蝶蘭，更名為「蘭嶼」，是台灣第二大離
島。

蘭花（tamek， 大麼可或日語kochozang，姑就浪）：現為瀕臨絕種、強制
保育的植物。

珠光鳳蝶、白鼻心（pahabahad，巴阿巴愛的或votdak，夫的大可、
panganpen，巴安笨）：詳見「部落百寶盒：與自然共舞的特殊生態」。

角鴞（totowo，杜杜霧）：即是俗稱的「貓頭鷹」；詳見「部落百寶盒：與
自然共舞的特殊生態」。

有一天，身體強壯又高大的希‧蓋雷提，將島上的人全都集合起來，並大聲宣布：「我叫希‧蓋雷提，我要將天空再舉高一點，因為它太矮了。」

於是，他就把天空舉得高高的，沒有人能夠摸得到。

還有一位叫做希‧杷吉拉勞的人，每當他看到胖嘟嘟的小孩和懷孕的婦女，就有一股想要吃掉他們的衝動。

不僅如此，這裡古古怪怪的人還很多。

自從古怪的人來到這座美麗的小島之後，島上的樹木和植物不再茂盛，鳥兒也不再快樂的歌唱了。過不久，來了一場大洪水，淹沒了這座島嶼以及這群古怪的人。

九年之後，天上的人讓這座小島再度浮出水面，漸漸的又開始長滿了樹木和其他生物，天上的人為了增添島上的美麗，再次賞賜了珍貴的植物蘭花、可愛的動物角鴞，以及美麗的珠光鳳蝶。

天上的人看到這裡又恢復了生機，於是降下祂的兩個孩子，吩咐一個孩子降在漁人部落的大石頭中，叫做石生人；另一個孩子則降在紅頭部落的竹子裡，叫做竹生人。

天上的人還賜給竹生人和石生人一項神力，就是他們身體的任何一個部位都可生下男孩或女孩。不過，當他們各自生下一男一女之後，就不再具有

 What's more?

船：達悟族人製作的拼板舟稱為tatala，音同「大大臘」，而不是由達悟族人製作的其他船都稱avang，音同「阿放」。

鬼（anito，阿尼杜）：達悟族人對「阿尼杜」的定義可以分成兩部分：1. 死去的人的總稱。2. 魔鬼。

希‧巴雷（Si-paloy）：人名。達悟族人對未婚者的稱呼，通常在名字前都以「Si」為開頭，例如「Si-naban」（希‧南邦）。

神力，成為完完全全的凡人了。

日子漸漸過去，天上的人賦予這兩個孩子身上的神力都應驗了。降在紅頭部落竹子裡的竹生人，順利的生下了一男一女，長大成人之後便結婚生子。奇怪的是，他們生下來的孩子不是眼睛瞎掉，就是身體畸形、智商低，養不活、長不大。

降在漁人部落巨石中的石生人，他的孩子也發生同樣的情形。

有一天，竹生人和石生人不約而同的去海邊釣魚時，恰巧在路上碰到，他們聊起了發生在孩子及孫子身上的事，經過一番討論之後，決定將雙方的兒女相互嫁娶，看看能不能夠改善現在這種情況。

事隔多年，果然如竹生人和石生人所期待的，之後生下的孩子個個聰明又有才幹，身體也非常健康，讓他們感到非常欣慰。

於是，竹生人和石生人便將智慧、知識及技藝傳授給下一代，教導女子種植地瓜、芋頭、辨識植物和織布，教導男人捕魚及協助女人開墾，更重要的是如何保護這座美麗的島嶼。

 What's more?

漁人（Iratay，伊然待）：指現今台東縣蘭嶼鄉的漁人部落。

紅頭（Imowrod，伊木入的）：指現今台東縣蘭嶼鄉的紅頭部落。

生小孩（amyan do vahey，阿米安 杜 發愛）：故事中提到竹生人和石生人的每個部位都可以生小孩，但另有一種說法是當摩擦膝蓋後才可以生出小孩。在達悟族人的觀念中，孩子出生後最好在清晨時命名並給予祝福，因為日出代表好的開始。

結婚（misin mo，米辛目）：由男女雙方父母挑選吉日舉行結婚儀式，男方穿禮服、戴金鍊、手環、銀盔及佩刀，清晨到女方家迎娶，雙方共享芋頭及豬肉。

芋頭（sosoli，書書立）：指水芋；在蘭嶼大多數人都栽種水芋。

竹生人和石生人還語重心長的交代：「千萬不可以浪費，只要取適量的資源，別糟蹋了造物者所賜予我們的一切。」

之後，他們為了保有這座美麗的島嶼，立下了許多規範做為管理島上的依據，並將這座小島命名為「碰書 奴 達悟」，也就是「人之島」的意思。

Where did it come from?

本故事採集自台東縣蘭嶼鄉漁人部落，由現年78歲的
鍾老太太（Si-yapen Maraos 希・雅芬・瑪拉烏絲）口述。

 What's more?

織布（tominon，都米奴問）：織布代表女性在社會上的地位，達悟族女人通常在秋冬的時候織衣。

造物者（ni mangamawog a tao，尼 媽阿媽五可 阿 達悟）：達悟族人的先知，非指基督。

碰書 奴 達悟（bongso no tao，碰書 奴 達悟）：意指人所居住的島嶼。

飛魚之神

月亮高掛的夜裡，飛魚被達悟族人手持的火光誘
惑，一隻隻跳進拼板舟裡。又到了蘭嶼獨有的飛
魚季節，達悟族人曾經因為不懂得飛魚習性，吃
後全身奇癢難治，幸好飛魚之神託夢給族中長
老，教會食用方法。從此，達悟族人不但謹守知
足常樂的道理，更珍惜海洋中的一切。

達悟族人的祖先靠著在海邊捕魚、挖貝類，以及在山上種地瓜、芋頭，維持三餐溫飽；他們由衷感謝造物者的恩賜，讓他們遠離挨餓受苦。

達悟族人住在四面環海的蘭嶼，對於海洋有著濃厚的情感，而在海洋中悠游的眾多魚類之中，唯獨對飛魚情有獨鍾。

能夠展翅飛翔的飛魚，傳說中是飛魚之神送給達悟族人的禮物。不過，達悟族人卻將飛魚和其他食物混合煮來吃，結果身上長滿了瘡，又癢又難治，於是決定再也不吃飛魚。

飛魚之神看見達悟族人捕捉飛魚之後，竟然不知道該如何食用，十分難過，為了讓達悟族人明白造物者創造的每一樣東西都是最尊貴的，便想了一個巧妙的方法，引導達悟族人正確食用飛魚。

於是，飛魚之神託夢給長老：「我是飛魚之神，我要你吩咐族人，從今天起遵守我所說的每一句話、每一項規則、每一個細節。你們要愛惜飛魚，不要浪費造物者的贈與，要尊重飛魚，不要讓我傷心、難過。」

What's more?

祖先（inapo，伊那布）：達悟族人沒有掃墓習俗，只有在每年十一月左右，利用祭神時順便祭拜往生親人。

飛魚（alibangbang，阿立棒棒）：達悟族人將飛魚分為下列4種：

1. 白翅飛魚：最早到蘭嶼附近海域的飛魚，牠們最喜歡亮光，是飛魚季節主要捕捉的魚種。

2. 紅翅飛魚：數量多，鰭上有黃褐色斑點，孕婦不能吃，否則會生出容易長痱子的嬰兒。

3. 黑翅飛魚：數量不多，在達悟族人眼中視為珍貴又偉大的飛魚，不可以用火烤食，否則會長瘡。

4. 紫斑鰭飛魚：數量最多，也是達悟族人的最愛；體型較小，小孩子可以吃。

「對不起，我們並非有意對飛魚不敬，只不過我們吃了飛魚之後，身上都會長滿了瘡，又癢又難治。」長老充滿愧疚的回說。

飛魚之神回答：「現在，我將如何食用飛魚的方法告訴你，你們就不會得皮膚病，要牢牢記住我所說的每一句話，絕對不可以遺漏，因為這也關係到你們族人世世代代的生活與規範。」

長老聽了之後便說：「您儘管說，我會牢記在心，並轉告要族人遵守。」

飛魚之神開始交代：「每年的飛魚季來臨時，要舉行祭飛魚的儀式，女人要上山挖地瓜、芋頭；男人要上山砍木材，製作飛魚架。季節到來的那一天，男人、女人都要分配工作，互相分工，並虔誠祝禱，祈求飛魚能夠豐收，保佑族人度過每一次海流或意外，大家平安、健康。」

What's more?

飛魚之神（mizezyaka libangbang，米樂拉可 立棒棒）：指會說話的飛魚。傳說中，飛魚之神教導達悟族人如何捕食飛魚的種種規定。

身上會長瘡之說：在達悟族的神話傳說故事中，飛魚不可以和其他魚一起混煮；也不可以任意烤來吃，若違反了這些規定，身上就會長瘡（皮膚病之類）。

長老（kamanrarakeh，嘎曼熱熱各）：達悟族中沒有頭目制，社會平等無階級之別，遇有大事或發生糾紛時，由各部落長老聚會商討；部落中雖然沒有明確的領導人，但具有特殊才能者例如擅用刀斧、手藝奇佳者等等，常被視為暫時性領導人。

飛魚季（mirayon，米然又安）：時間在國曆三到六月份；詳見「部落百寶盒：飛魚季節來臨了」。

飛魚架（zazawan，拉拉萬）：枯枝搭成的架子，用來曬飛魚乾。

捕飛魚（mitawaz so libangbang，米大襪了 書 立棒棒）：方法是在夜裡搭乘拼板舟，一人拿著一枝點燃的枯樹枝，飛魚看見火光，會向著光源撲來，這時就可網住魚群。

「當丈夫下海捕飛魚時，妻子要捉陸蟹來慰勞丈夫的辛苦；而丈夫要將捕回來的飛魚，煮給妻子和孩子們吃。飛魚實在太多時，全家人要共同將魚處理乾淨，然後將飛魚曬乾儲存起來。丈夫要吩咐妻子、孩子，在食用飛魚時不可拿到外頭吃；吃飽後要跟大家說：『我吃飽了，大家請慢用。』用完餐之後一定要洗手。」飛魚之神耐心的交代每一項細節。

「飛魚季節裡，禁止說不吉祥或罵人的話，也不能捕捉或釣其他的魚類，而且捕飛魚時不能太貪心，只要捕足一年的份量就可以了。」

「飛魚季節過完之後，家家戶戶用歌聲、舞蹈，來慶祝豐收與平安。要在歡喜之日，將地瓜、芋頭、魚乾分給親朋好友共享，尤其是孤單的老人或無法出海的人家。這樣你們的族人才會年年有魚吃，同時在相互幫助之下，子子孫孫才會延續到永遠。」

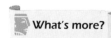
What's more?

陸蟹（teyngi，的人尼）：飛魚季節中，女人不可隨便離家，必須準備飛魚祭的祭品及宴食，並挖陸蟹來慰勞辛苦捕魚的男人。

達悟族的用餐禮儀：一定得從最年長者至晚輩一一稱呼完畢，之後有禮貌的說：「我吃飽了，謝謝！」

跳舞（maganam，媽嘎那門）：男子的「勇士舞」，身著丁字褲，上身露出結實肌肉，原始的吼聲帶動整齊有力的舞步，時蹲時跳時旋轉；女子的「頭髮舞」，身著白底藍黑紋相間的服飾，又唱又跳，低下頭去再抬起，長髮隨之飄逸，宛如海浪。

不能出海的人家：喪家及殘障人士不能出海。

達悟族吃魚的文化：男人、老人、女人各吃不同的魚，是過去利用有限物資留下來的生活智慧。男人吃的魚叫做「rahet」（然俄）；原則上老人什麼魚都可以吃，而老人吃的魚叫做「angsa」（盎沙阿），例如鬼頭刀；女人吃的魚叫做「oyod」（烏悠的），像是肉質細嫩的石斑魚，尤其懷孕及哺乳期間需要較多的營養，所以女人吃的魚比較講究。不過，因為時代變遷，物資充裕，已經不再這樣做區別。

飛魚之神說完之後，長老就醒過來了，他從臥房起身坐在屋外的靠背石上，面向著海洋，不斷的思索著飛魚之神託給自己的夢。長老心裡想著，飛魚之神說的話很有道理，怎麼可浪費海洋贈與的任何恩賜？

飛魚祭的由來。每年達悟族人舉行的飛魚祭，象徵著對每一個生命的尊重、對大自然的愛，以及對造物者的敬畏。

Where did it come from?

本故事採集自台東縣蘭嶼鄉東清部落，由宋金庭女士（Si-yapen Pazpazen 希‧雅芬‧姑誕）口述。

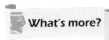 **What's more?**

靠背石（panadngan，巴那的案）：靠背石指的是達悟族傳統家屋前，在庭院中兩塊長長直立的扁平石頭，這兩塊石頭就像椅子的靠背，族人常坐在庭院中背靠著石頭，乘涼休息或聊天。

達悟拼板舟

> 達悟族人沿著神秘水洞，來到地底人的世界，眼前景象令人既驚又喜。
>
> 男女和諧分工、生活井然有序，尤其精緻的大船讓族人大開眼界。地底人傾囊相授造船技術，也讓達悟族人了解：善用資源、互助合作、回饋共享的心意，才是造船成功的關鍵。

有一隻非常聰明又可愛的老鼠，他是地底人的化身，被天上的人派到達悟族人居住的地方。

地底人和達悟族人都是海洋民族，生活方式一樣，所以很能夠相互溝通。

達悟族人對造船的領悟力雖然高，但仍比不上精通造船技術的地底人。達悟族人每次到海邊網魚時，不但捕獲量很少，船隻還常常進水，所以天上的人決定差派地底人──老鼠，到達悟族人居住的地方，教導達悟族人造船技術。

地底人來到達悟族人居住的部落，跟當地的達悟族人相處融洽，也交換了許多生活意見。過了一段時間之後，老鼠便帶領著十二名達悟族人，沿著水洞，到地底人的家鄉去。

「哇！好多人，比我們的族人還要多。」

第一次到地底人的家鄉，達悟族人既興奮又好奇，忍不住東張西望。他們發現這群地底人生活十分和諧、快樂，女人種地瓜、芋頭、織布，男人專心伐木和研究造船技術，他們建造的船既漂亮又先進。

但是，他們說話的聲音卻是：「旺、旺、旺！」好奇怪哦！

一位較年長的地底人，親切又友善的歡迎著達悟族人來訪，並帶領達悟族人認識他們的文化和生活方式。

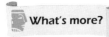 **What's more?**

造船（mitatala，米大大臘）：詳見「部落百寶盒：達悟拼板舟的製造方式」。

水洞（tozngan no ranom，都了阿安 奴 讓奴門）：目前，島上尚未找到傳說中的這個水洞。

傳授造船技術：有另一種說法是地底人化身為老鼠，吸引達悟族小孩進入地界，學習新事物，從中領悟造船技術。

地底人的長老對達悟族人說：「我們的生活是共有共享，最討厭自私的人，我們喜歡合力完成一項工作。」

「祖先教訓我們不能過度砍伐山林，因為一旦山林被破壞了，不但會帶來水土的災難，我們也將沒有木頭打造堅固的船，更無法出海捕撈豐盛的漁獲。」

「在海中捕魚一定要適量，夠家人吃就可以了。我們會選擇較良好的土地種植地瓜、芋頭，當做主要的食物來源，並拿來做為祭儀中的祭品。這就是我們地底人和你們最大的不同吧！」

地底人的長老逐一說明自己族人的生活方式。

達悟族人聽了地底人的長老一席話，非常敬佩他們對環境的愛護和利用，也認為只有確實保護山林、土地及海洋，才能為後代子孫留下美好的環境。

「請問你們是如何打造出這麼堅固的船？」很想增進造船技術的達悟族人進一步問。

地底人的長老微笑的說：「我會親自帶領你們去看我們族人是如何造船的。」

接著，達悟族人提出造船時遇到的難題：「我們不管怎麼造船，船還是容易損壞；不但使用的時間很短，航向海洋時也不十分順利，船身總是不平衡。」

地底人的長老回答：「要造一艘美麗又堅固的船不容易，我們也曾經和你們有同樣的遭遇。後來，天上的人告訴我們的祖先：『造船所需要的一切

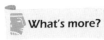
What's more?

土地（karatayan，嘎拉達宴）：達悟族每個部落各自擁有漁場、牧地、農地，其他部落的居民不能擅自進入或使用。

都取自於大自然，必須尊重造物者和我們所居住的大自然，才能合乎造物者的心意。」於是，天上的人就將造船的技術和注意事項告訴我們的祖先，我們世世代代便按照天上的人所傳授的技巧去造船。」

地底人還不忘叮囑達悟族人：「造船是一件非常莊嚴又神聖的事情，需要男女分工合作才能完成。」

於是，地底人吩咐達悟族女人：「你們女人要勤勞耕種，種植地瓜、芋頭、山藥、小米時，記得隨時拔除雜草，種植的東西才會繁茂碩大。至於飼養豬、羊，女人也要多費心，因為牠們都是祭船儀式中必備的祭品，之後還要分送給親朋好友當禮物。」

接著，地底人告訴達悟族男人說：「你們男人要幫助女人開墾，好讓她們可以耕種，因為她們種植的東西都是造船完成時，舉行祭船儀式的必需品，這是非常重要的。」

地底人帶著達悟族人來到造船的地方，好幾組人正在努力的共同建造艘美麗的船。

一位領導者向達悟族人說明造船的方法與技術：「造船時必須遵守禁忌：

第一，為了尊重山林，造船之前，族人一定要彼此商量，並由較年長且較有經驗的人來選擇船身的材料。

第二，不能說罵人或不吉祥的話，以免影響漁獲。

 What's more?

達悟族人的喪葬習俗：通常喪家會用木條將家屋圍起來，送葬路線也會用兩排木條區隔開來。墓地通常位在部落左邊靠海的地方。

成員（yami keyteytetngehan，亞米 給特地的安）：達悟族人過去固定三或六年造一艘大船，如果勤於保養，使用壽命可長達六年。

第三，造船成員中，若有人遭遇不幸或家人有喪事時，應該停止工作，以表示悼念。」

「當船造好之後，要舉行下水儀式，將你們所種植的地瓜、芋頭盛滿船身，並用家畜的血來祭船，大家唱歌、跳舞來祭祀，這樣才能帶來更多的福氣和幸運。同時，也要宴請親朋好友，來共享這美好的祭典。」這名領導者詳細交代新船完成後的祭儀。

達悟族人記取了地底人所傳授的技巧和吩咐之後，就帶著他們贈送的地瓜、芋頭、豬、羊等等，回到居住的部落，並分享這一切。從此，達悟族人結合自己的經驗和地底人所傳授的技巧，重新建立屬於自己的生活與文化，並造出船身線條美麗又堅固實用的拼板舟。

不過，不知道為什麼，祖先留下來的傳說就再也沒有關於地底人的任何消息或故事了。

Where did it come from?

本故事採集自台東縣蘭嶼鄉東清部落，由鄭貴生先生（Si-yapen Pazpazen 席·亞分·巴倫巴嫩）口述。

What's more?

下水儀式（yamapalwas，亞媽巴路娃絲）：詳見「部落百寶盒：大船下水祭」。

祭血（rala，讓辣）：通常是用豬或雞的血。

分享（masipangarilow，媽西巴阿熱路）：達悟族人喜歡分享，尤其常將魚乾、地瓜、芋頭互相饋贈。

拼板舟（tatala no tao，他他拉 奴 達悟）：達悟族是海洋民族，船舟是捕魚的交通工具，所以過去的男子必須學會造船技術，否則無法在達悟族的社會中立足。詳見「部落百寶盒：達悟拼板舟的製造方式」。

林投樹下的男孩

林投樹底下傳來嚎啕大哭的嬰兒哭聲，還好上
天憐憫，被老夫婦收養。長大後的他，勤勞又
孝順，直到生母來相認，才知道真相。

他舉辦達悟族最隆重的筵席，挑選肥又結實的
豬、羊，邀請老夫婦及生母一起享用。

男孩不但知恩圖報感謝老夫婦，又化解對親生
母親的恨意，誠為可貴。

達悟族部落裡，有一個男孩非常聰明、可愛、善良、孝順，不過他的身世背後卻有一段不尋常的故事。

幾年前，有一個年輕女孩還沒有結婚就懷孕了，部落裡的人都懷疑這位女孩做了不該做的事，人人都不願意接近她。

當年輕女孩知道部落裡的人都對她起疑心且議論紛紛時，便十分害怕在大白天出門走動，只敢趁著黑夜出門。

年輕女孩的肚子漸漸的隆起來了，她更害怕出門，小心翼翼的把自己隱藏起來。

當孩子即將降臨人世時，年輕女孩偷偷的躲在沒人知道的地方生產，生下了一個白白胖胖的小男嬰，眼睛水汪汪的非常可愛，可是因為孩子沒有爸爸，年輕女孩害怕部落裡的人不歡迎她可愛的孩子，便決定請媽媽在黑夜裡，將小男嬰丟棄。

年輕女孩的媽媽，在離部落很遠且長滿了林投樹的地方，丟下了小男嬰。

在部落裡的另一處，住著一對恩愛的老夫婦，他們結婚多年都無法懷孕，非常渴望有個小孩，可是老天就是不賜給他們。

同一天夜裡，老先生在前往海邊撒網捕魚的路上，走呀，走呀，當他慢慢的走近林投樹時，突然聽到林中傳來「哇哇！」的哭叫聲，他好奇的朝著

What's more?

嬰兒：還未命名前，都叫做kekey（哥給）。達悟族的命名方式是親從子名制，男女婚後生育頭胎，父母親必須放棄本名，父親改稱「Siaman-○○○」（夏曼‧○○○），母親改稱「Sinan-○○○」（希南‧○○○），後面加上孩子名。

林投樹（ango，阿奴）：是一種多年生常綠的大型灌木，多為一大片群聚生長；葉子邊緣及葉背面都有硬鋸齒，相當刺人。蘭嶼島上現在還有很多林投樹，達悟族人常利用氣根部分製作魚繩來曬魚乾。

發出聲音的方向走去，發現樹底下竟然躺了個小男嬰 。老先生又驚又喜，卻不禁為這可愛的小男嬰嘆息：「唉，這麼可愛的孩子，是誰這麼狠心將他遺棄在這多刺的林投樹下呢？」

老先生憐惜的抱起小男嬰，將他摟在懷中帶回家。老先生一回到家，開心的對妻子說：「老伴呀！我今天沒有去網魚，因為我在林投樹下撿到了這個可愛的小男嬰。」

妻子看到小男嬰也萬分歡喜：「這真是老天賜給我們的禮物啊！」

老先生不忘吩咐妻子：「妳要多喝開水，才能有母奶給小孩子喝。」

這對老夫婦瞞著部落裡的人，小心翼翼的把小男嬰扶養長大。

當小男嬰漸漸的長大，在庭院裡活蹦亂跳時，左鄰右舍都覺得非常奇怪，部落裡的人都這麼傳著：「奇怪了！這對夫妻結婚多年都沒有生小孩，現在他們老了，怎麼跑出了個小孩呢？」

長大後的小男孩，常常去海邊釣魚供家裡吃，也幫年邁的老夫婦上山開墾，種地瓜和芋頭。

可是，當他和部落裡的孩子一起玩的時候，一些孩子都嘲笑他：「你不是你爸媽親生的，你是從林投樹下撿回來的孩子。」

他聽了非常氣憤，每次被逼急了，便大聲回答：「我是媽媽親生的，而且我是喝媽媽的奶水長大的，我的爸媽非常疼我。」

所以，每當有人跟小男孩說同樣的話，他都會和對方大吵一架，然後回家問母親，母親總是以溫柔但堅定的口吻安慰他：「孩子，你當然是我的寶貝兒子。」聽了母親的話，小男孩安心多了。

小男孩一年比一年成熟懂事，很勤勞的分擔家事，但部落裡依然有人嚷

嚷：「他不是老夫婦的小孩。」現在，無論如何，他都不再因此感到困擾或動怒了。

轉眼間，小男孩長大了，相貌英俊又懂事，他跟往常一樣到海邊去釣魚，到山上採芋頭、地瓜，餵養家畜。

有一天，年輕男孩照往常一樣上山耕種，途中遇到了一位看起來很面熟的中年婦人，婦人迎面而來開口便說：「孩子！你是我的孩子呀！我是你的母親！」

「我不是你的孩子，我媽媽在家呢！」年輕男孩大聲否認，心中卻充滿疑惑。

這位婦人不死心，每次看見年輕男孩就纏著他。

年輕男孩受不了這位婦人的糾纏，回家後忍不住再問母親：「媽媽！我是不是您親生的孩子呀？為什麼總有一位婦人對我糾纏不休呢？」

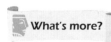

What's more?

成熟（maka veyvow，馬嘎 飛付）：達悟族沒有特定的成年儀式，而是以能夠獨立做事來斷定是否成年，像是男孩可以釣魚或捕魚，以及參與部落裡的大大小小事，而女孩要會做家事、種地瓜及芋頭、捉螃蟹等等。

豬、羊：達悟族人的豬隻都養在家屋四周，隨便讓牠們漫遊覓食，只有少數家庭擁有豬圈；山羊則全部自行覓食，羊主可在部落牧地裡隨意放牧，從羊耳朵上的記號來辨別所有權，不怕被偷。達悟族人養家畜目的並非供日常食用，而是在節慶及祭儀時才會宰殺。

吉祥的日子（apiya vehan，阿比亞 飛安）：達悟族人的吉祥日子，指的是月圓或清早。

母親拭去眼角的淚水，看著當年從林投樹下抱回來的年輕男孩說：「我的孩子，你長大了，事到如今，我不再瞞你，因為你已經可獨立自主了。」養育年輕男孩多年的老夫婦，便將他的身世一五一十的告訴他。

在達悟族的社會裡，宰殺豬、羊宴請親友是一件最光榮的事，也是孝敬父母的最好表現。

年輕男孩為了報答這對老夫婦的養育之恩，於是在吉祥的日子裡，挑選了又大又肥又結實的豬、羊來宰殺，並同時宴請親朋好友一起前來。

年輕男孩也邀請了親生母親來共享，可是，他將又少又小的肉給她，而把又肥大又好吃的肉分給了養育他多年的老夫婦。

Where did it come from?
本故事採集自台東縣蘭嶼鄉漁人部落，由現年78歲的鍾老太太（Si-yapen Maraos 希·雅芬·瑪拉烏絲）口述。

部落百寶盒║傳授哈「原」秘笈，搖身變成達悟通

一、愛好和平的達悟族

達悟族是台灣唯一住在離島的原住民，他們的家位於台灣東南方的太平洋小島上，就是蘭嶼。達悟族又稱為雅美族（Yami），「雅美」一詞是日本人統治時的稱呼，也是目前政府官方的稱法；「達悟」（Tao）的語意是「人」，現在蘭嶼人都以達悟族自稱。

▶ 和其他台灣原住民族大不同

達悟族人相信他們的祖先來自菲律賓，研究也發現，達悟語言和菲律賓北方的巴丹島居民相當雷同；此外，蘭嶼的拼板舟和半穴居，也可能來自巴丹島。由此可見，達悟族人和菲律賓的巴丹島人關係很深。在二〇〇二年七月，有一群達悟族人曾遠赴巴丹島，舉辦一趟跨海尋根之旅，希望與巴丹島彼此定期交流歷史、文化、語言等等。

展現在文化方面，達悟族有明顯不同於其他台灣原住民族之處，他們沒有釀酒技術、也不紋身，但是獨有的冶金工藝，尤其是男子銀盔和黃金飾片，非常具有特色。另外，達悟族人沒有獵頭習俗，也不使用弓箭，雖然有武器，但多用於攻擊惡靈，而非對抗敵人。因為蘭嶼島上人口稀少，如果互相獵首、彼此仇視，將危害族群生存。

現在，蘭嶼雖然也有民選鄉長及村長，擁有行政上的領導權；不過，每個部落仍有屬於自己的社會權威與社會機能，所以部落內的紛爭大都能以傳統方式解決，若非必要，達悟族人很少會上鄉公所或是警察局。

▶ 核廢料是惡靈

生性愛好和平的達悟族人，卻因為不滿核廢料的處理決策而憤怒。

一九八〇年，當時的政府告訴達悟族人，要在蘭嶼興建魚罐頭工廠，但是完工之後，不見有人來收購漁獲，只見運來一艘又一艘的貨櫃。十幾年後，達悟族人才明白，那根本不是魚罐頭工廠，而是核廢料儲存場。核廢料埋在蘭嶼土地，成為達悟族人眼中最可怕的惡靈，為了保護自己的家園，以及蘭嶼

原有的生態環境，達悟族人多次向政府提出嚴正抗議，要求必須將核廢料儲存場遷出蘭嶼；達悟族人可說是台灣反核的前哨站。

二、與自然共舞的特殊生態

蘭嶼氣候濕熱多雨，島上動植物種類繁多，其中不少是全球特有品種，比較知名的有珠光鳳蝶、蘭嶼角鴞、綠蠵龜，以及在四周海域分布的多種珊瑚。蘭嶼兼具自然與人文之美，已被文建會列為我國十一個世界遺產之首，並正向聯合國教科文組織爭取列入世界文化遺址。以下將介紹幾種動植物，讓大家了解。

▶ 蘭嶼野百合（vonitan，夫尼旦）

又名鐵砲百合，有「可以一片片剝下」之意，花朵全身潔白，花瓣有六片，前端像喇叭，散發出清新香味，達悟族人視為冬天即將結束，春天就快到來的季節性指標植物。在台灣北部和東部、澎湖、綠島和蘭嶼，都可見到她優雅的身影。

▶ 珠光鳳蝶（pahabahad，巴阿巴愛的）

象徵人類的靈魂，達悟族人相信人死後，靈魂會附著在蝴蝶身上。珠光鳳蝶因為在陽光下會散發出珍珠般的光芒而得名，有台灣最美麗的蝴蝶之稱，也是全台體型最大的蝴蝶，只有蘭嶼才有；近年來，因人為破壞、食物短缺與非法濫捕，數量銳減面臨絕種，是世界公告保育昆蟲之一。

▶ 蘭嶼角鴞（totowo，杜杜霧）

俗稱「貓頭鷹」，正出自牠的叫聲，是一種夜行性動物，身長約二十公分，目前數量不到一千隻。老一輩的達悟族人相信蘭嶼角鴞是惡靈的化身，而牠們又喜歡棲息在達悟族人認為不吉祥的棋盤腳樹枝上。

▶ 綬帶鳥

綬帶鳥是蘭嶼特有鳥，最顯眼的就是一對像綬帶似的長尾羽，身長可達三十五公分。雌雄鳥都有亮藍色眼圈及嘴喙，鳴叫聲高亢宏亮，飛行時拖曳著長尾羽，姿態極為優美。也因為這兩片尾羽，好像梁山伯帽子的綸巾，也有人稱牠「梁山伯」。綬帶鳥棲息在蘭嶼的原始森林中，不過近年來快速開發及人為干擾，目前也面臨了生存上的危機。

▶ 白鼻心（votdak，夫的大可，或panganpen，巴安笨）

俗稱果子狸，屬於保育類動物，從額頭到鼻樑有條明顯白紋是其特徵，模樣相當可愛。不過在達悟族人眼中，牠可是魔鬼所飼養的動物。

▶ 綠蠵龜

俗名石龜，台灣地區除蘭嶼以外，只有澎湖望安島是較穩定的產卵地，這些地方都已經公告為野生動物保護區。每年五至十月是綠蠵龜產卵季，母龜會上岸選擇適當海灘，先挖洞產卵後，再撥土埋卵，然後游回大海；龜卵大約五十天左右孵化，小海龜趁夜傾巢而出，藉由星光導引，爬向大海。若有人工光源，很可能會讓小海龜迷失方向，爬向陸地而死，所以在綠蠵龜產卵季節，請不要打擾，也千萬別拿著手電筒在海灘亂照哦。

三、傳統的半穴屋與新屋禮

蘭嶼有種老房子，一半在地上，一半在地下，稱為「半穴屋」。

由於蘭嶼屬於熱帶海洋性氣候，大部分的時候都很炎熱，再加上颱風每年來襲，島上沒有高山屏障；面對這樣的環境，達悟族人發展出獨特的半穴屋：用石頭和木材在背風的坡地上蓋房子，一部分建築在地上、一部分在地下，不只防風還可以防曬。尤其，因為地下部分有土層，隔熱效果絕佳，整個室內十分涼爽，而且穴居結構堅固，即使颱風來襲也高枕無憂。

▶ 主屋面向大海

傳統的達悟房子有主屋、工作房和涼台；主屋包括客廳和臥房，深入地下二到三公尺處，由於房子一半在地下，為了避免淹水，必須挖排水溝。主屋面向大海，從地上只能看見覆蓋著茅草的屋頂，是日常生活及舉行儀式的場所，室內昏暗，空間不大，多數人家會在牆上掛羊角、戰袍和盔甲，以彰顯威望。屋外涼台專供乘涼休息及聊天社交，工作房則是工作場所，族人多半在裡面從事編織、製作木器戰甲或冶煉金銀鐵器等工作。

▶ 分享禮芋和禮肉

達悟族人蓋房子是不請工人的，而是親朋好友得知消息後，主動前來幫忙，這種互助合作的精神是蘭嶼社會的一大特色。除了互助，達悟族人也愛好分享，新屋落成後，屋主會舉行落成禮邀請親友一起慶祝，從大約三、四年前就要開始籌備，例如開闢大量的水芋田，並飼養大群豬羊，以便到時舉行儀式，可以有足夠的禮芋和禮肉分送親友。

在一九六六至一九八〇年，政府推行山地生活改進運動，為了改善達悟族人的生活，拆除半穴屋，興建鋼筋水泥樓房。達悟族人住在這些房子一段時間之後很不適應，尤其到了夏季，屋內宛如蒸籠。

達悟族人重新思考之後，認為還是傳統的半穴屋最適合族人的文化風俗與生活特性，所以在野銀和朗島部落還保存部分的半穴屋。目前，蘭嶼島上傳統住屋雖已逐漸被鋼筋水泥建築取代，但是舉行新屋落成禮的習俗卻從未改變。

四、飛魚季節來臨了

達悟族人認為飛魚是天神恩賜的禮物。每年二月初達悟族人便開始「招飛魚」，因為三月開始飛魚會隨著黑潮洄游到蘭嶼海域，之後將展開為期好幾個月的捕飛魚活動；國曆三至六月的「飛魚季」，是蘭嶼島上最忙碌的季節。

在捕撈飛魚的季節，達悟族人會舉行「飛魚祭」。「飛魚祭」大致可分三個階段，首先是出動大船的儀式，其次為小船的儀式，最後是結束飛魚季節的儀式；全部祭典包括大船招魚祭、大船初漁祭、小船招魚祭、小船初漁祭、飛魚乾收藏祭及飛魚終食祭。

▶ 飛魚回來哦！

大船招魚祭都在清晨舉行，這天達悟族男人要盛裝，將大船推到海邊參與祭拜，每艘船都要坐滿人，代表福氣圓滿。等到全部落男人到齊之後，領祭者宣布飛魚季中的禁忌與捕魚規則，然後高唱頌詞，接著以銀盔、水瓢或手勢，帶領所有船組成員面向大海呼喊「飛魚回來哦！」祈求飛魚快快回來。之後殺雞，將雞血分給參與祭典的每位男子，大家以食指沾雞血輕點海邊黑色卵石，象徵漁獲將和石頭一樣長久；再取出祭雞的內臟，從肝膽來判定今年飛魚季的運氣及船組安危。

午餐完畢稍做休息，船員們再回到海邊，這時候領祭者會撿五顆卵石到船主家前，放在曬魚架與四根支柱之下，並且搖晃著，象徵魚架因掛滿了飛魚而晃動，以祈求豐收。

當招魚祭之後，首輪新月出現時，船組才開始出海捕飛魚。首先，在船上點燃枯樹枝照耀海面，以吸引飛魚靠近，再用漁網捕撈，這是集體捕撈階段。至於個人捕撈，則必須等到小船招魚祭以後才可以。不過，近年來引進機動船筏，大船已逐漸被取代；傳統夜間點火把誘魚的方式也幾乎難得一見，已經改成開機動船在日間牽網撈捕了。

▶ 飛魚乾收藏祭與終食祭

達悟族人對飛魚觀察入微，並依來到的時間、數量多寡、體型大小等，決定捕食方法。例如在三月時，一個船組只有一位捕漁夫，用一道漁網捕魚；四月下旬，海象逐漸平穩，飛魚增多，大小船隻會不分晝夜出海，用多道漁網捕捉；五月下旬到飛魚季結束，船員用個人工具獵魚，所有的漁獲由船組成員平均分配。近年來，由於年輕人紛紛到台灣工作，使得留在部落的人必須打破原有船組方式捕魚，集資買漁網共同使用，再一同分享漁獲，這已成為蘭嶼新興的捕魚方式。

等到飛魚汛期結束時，六到七月會舉行飛魚乾收藏祭，把捕獲的飛魚曬乾儲存以備冬天食用。結束捕飛魚的當天，部落會將今年捕獲的大魚（通常是鮪魚）尾巴穿串吊掛在海邊，從那天起，不再捕捉飛魚，而改捉其他魚類。

目前，達悟族的飛魚乾收藏祭多和小米豐收祭合辦，時間大約在六月下旬。當天早上，親戚們會互相贈送禮物，通常是芋頭及魚乾；中午家家戶戶團聚共餐，餐後進行搗小米活動，邊搗邊唱歌，木臼中滿滿的小米象徵來年一樣豐足。下午各船組將大船推回船屋收藏，宣示飛魚季結束。

每年中秋節過後，就是舉行「飛魚終食祭」的時候了，族人們紛紛穿上禮服，戴上手環，用餐前以禮語答謝神的賜予，並盡量把飛魚乾吃完，祈求年年有飛魚。

五、達悟拼板舟的製造方式

飛魚季的蘭嶼，海邊隨處可見大小船隻。達悟族人造船技術世界一流，不用量尺與鐵釘，只用一把斧頭，把一塊塊木板拼接成一艘艘造型優美的拼板舟；和一般獨木舟僅由一根木頭挖鑿而成，完全不同。

▶ 結構特殊的拼板舟

達悟拼板舟分為大船及小船，大船有六人、八人或十人座，由二十七塊木板拼成。小船有一人、二人或三人座，由二十一塊木材拼成，大小船結構相同。

新船通常在每年六月建造，每造一艘大船，都是同一船組的大事。達悟族人認為船是男人身體的一部分，造船是神聖的使命，從選材到完成，大約需要半年的時間，但是船板樹材需經數十年培育，所以常常是父祖種樹、兒孫取材，造船技術一代傳一代。

達悟拼板舟的結構，中央是龍骨，分成舟首、舟底、舟尾三段，兩側為舷板，分成二至四層，每層三片，板與板間以木釘連接，細縫用巴洛樹根剝成的棉花狀物填充，防止滲水。舷板與龍骨接合時，必須全神貫注。

▶ 造船有很多禁忌

達悟族人會因船板所在位置與功用的不同，來選擇不同的造船材料。例如，漁船出海或入港時，都會在海邊拖拉摩擦，首尾常會碰撞礁石，因此龍骨必須選擇最堅硬、莖幹粗大、耐磨耐腐的樹種，通常是蕃龍眼或欖仁舅等樹木。船身第一層也要選用硬質樹材，第二到四層中間板則用較輕的木材即可，方便讓船身浮起。

新船完工後需上色或雕刻，達悟拼板舟除了黑、紅、白三色外，不能加入其他顏色。船身凹處要塗白色，凸處黑色，沒在水裡的船板則塗上紅色；如果預算不多，船身只要塗滿白色即可，也可免除舉辦下水儀式。

另外，為了避免招犯惡靈，船槳不可雕刻任何花紋，在繪製船身圖案時也要小心，不能觸犯禁忌。達悟族的傳統圖騰包括人、魚、海浪、三角紋、菱形紋和蛇形紋。最後，船的兩端彎曲處還要刻上齒輪狀圖案，象徵「船之眼」，有避邪作用。

▶ 大舟側面組合示意圖與取材說明

1. 舟尾龍骨
2. 舟首龍骨
3. 舟底龍骨
4. 第一層中間板
5. 靠近舟首、舟尾第一層板（二片）
6. 第二層中間板
7. 靠近舟首、舟尾第二層板（二片）
8. 第三層中間板
9. 靠近舟首、舟尾第三層板（二片）
10. 第四層中間板
11. 靠近舟首、舟尾第四層板（二片）
12. 舵槳架：放置舵槳用。

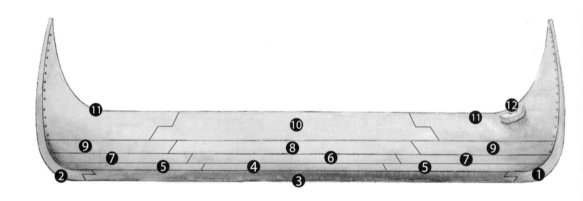

蕃龍眼　　欖仁舅　　蘭嶼赤楠

這些樹種耐磨又耐腐，樹材堅硬且厚實，多用來製作龍骨和舟底，可以發揮很好的鉛垂作用讓船身平穩。

綠島榕　　大葉山欖　　麵包樹

要讓船身浮在水面，需選用像麵包樹質輕的木材當做中間板。

小葉桑

多削成小木釘，
做為接合用。

1. 黑色：刮下鍋底的黑灰當成顏料。

2. 白色：利用貝殼粉當成顏料。

3. 船之眼：有避邪作用。

4. 傳統圖騰：包括人、魚、海浪 、三角
　 紋、菱形紋 、蛇形紋。

5. 紅色：利用紅土當成顏料。

六、大船下水祭

當大型雕刻拼板舟完成時，達悟族人習慣要舉行隆重的下水祭，一方面向船靈
祈禱，另一方面趕走惡靈，希望船隻下水後，能有豐碩的漁獲。

▶ 成堆的水芋覆蓋新船

舉行下水祭的前一天早上，船組將採收的水芋覆蓋在新船上，受邀的客人用歌聲讚美船主，船組則高唱迎賓歌；還沒唱完前，客人不可以坐下來，否則會得不到禮物。晚餐後，又開始歌唱，直到天明。隔天一早，船主會分送禮芋、禮肉給客人，等到中午，新船下水祭的重頭戲就要登場了。

大船首航前，全部落男子會穿著丁字褲，分成數路走向新船，行進間人人握拳、瞪目頓足，並高聲怒吼，一直重複同樣的動作，直到靠近船身後又繼續高唸咒文。接著，穿著盛裝的全體船員，頭戴銀盔、手拿長刀，坐在自己的船位上向船靈祈禱；緊接著船主走到船中央，揮舞長刀，驅趕惡靈，其他船員下船加入全部落男子之中，眾人握拳、用力抖動，大聲嘶吼，腳猛踩地面。達悟族人相信，臉孔越猙獰兇狠，越能驅走惡靈。

然後，進行拋船儀式，船員與其他成年男子合力將坐在新船裡的船主和新船一起拋到半空中，隨後抬起新船向海邊走去，並反覆做出驅逐惡靈的動作。到達海邊後，必須再進行試航儀式，所有人配合波浪起伏，緩緩的將新船拋舉入海，並由挑選出來的十名划水好手擔任試航，在近處海面繞行一圈回來後，才換該組船員上船，返航後再將船拖上岸。

▶ 期待漁獲滿載

等船上岸時，船主會將事先準備好的祭（雞）血，放在船尾右側供奉船靈，並站在新船上面向大海唸咒語，族人隨後一擁而上，用食指沾血塗在海邊卵石上，期盼招魚入港、漁獲滿載。

下午，船員會準備一盆最大最好的水芋配上五花肉，聚集到船主家。當晚船主也會煮雞和魚，分享給船員。隔天，船員再把船推到海邊，船主的妻子會身穿全套禮服，送來幸運祭品「小米」，象徵把十全十美的運氣交給船組。接著，新船再出海繞行一圈，大船下水祭才告圓滿完成。

達悟族傳統的大船下水祭，在新船建造機會減少後，已成為難得一見的景象了。

▶ 達悟傳統服飾圖解

1. 飾品：

通常用一些堅硬的材質，例如台東龍眼 、
烏心石、毛柿、薏苡及倒地鈴等果實，加上
鉛筆海膽、鸚鵡螺等串製而成。

2. 女子服飾：

主要以馬尼拉麻為材料，上身穿胸兜或背
心，下身穿附有繫帶的方布裙，所有織衣都
是白色為底，黑、藍紋相間。

3. 男子戰服：

包括蘭嶼赤楠製的木刀、水籐編的籐
盾、椰子葉鞘織的背甲，以及椰殼加山
林投製成的籐盔。

▶ 大船下水祭與達悟傳統服飾圖解

4. 男子服飾：　一般上身都穿無袖無領的短背心，配上丁字褲。丁字褲是丁字
帶纏繞而成的，多以瘤冠麻或落尾麻編織，方便上山下海，也
適合蘭嶼濕熱的氣候。達悟男子的第一件丁字褲，要選擇天氣
晴朗的吉祥日子，面向日出方向穿上，象徵永不分離。

5. 銀盔：　　　將銀元敲打成薄片重疊連結製成，盔前留一方孔，
可以看見外面，視為傳家寶物。

6. 堆芋儀式：　大船下水祭前幾天，婦女穿著禮服到田間挖取水芋；
在舉行時，要將水芋堆置在大船上，隨後分送親友。

7. 黑雞尾羽：　　在首尾的最高處插上黑雞尾羽，可保佑航行平安。

8. 男子禮服：　　頭戴銀盔、身著藍紋短上衣及丁字褲、頸戴黃金飾片、手持長
　　　　　　　　刀。達悟族人相信禮服具有特殊靈力，不但織衣時特別慎重，
　　　　　　　　穿著前還要以豬羊獻祭。

9. 黃金飾片：　　將黃金打成倒 8 字型，掛在頸上，象徵財富。

10. 女子禮服：　　頭戴木帽、身著藍紋披肩、下身穿裙子、頸上戴瑪瑙珠鍊、
　　　　　　　　手執鏤花掘芋棒。

造訪部落　部落藏寶圖，來挖達悟寶

看過了達悟族的神話與傳說故事，和達悟族人一起下海捕飛魚，感受獨特的大船祭儀式，覺得意猶未盡吧！

達悟族目前大約有三千多人，全部分布在台東縣蘭嶼鄉，主要有六個部落：紅頭、漁人、椰油三個部落在前山；朗島、東清、野銀三個部落在後山，每個部落都有固定的山林獵地、耕地和漁區。島上最高峰是紅頭山，海拔高度五百五十二公尺。現在，透過這份精心編製的「蘭嶼達悟族文化導覽圖」，陪伴身歷其境，盡情挖掘部落文化寶藏，保證不虛此行。

到蘭嶼旅遊既可以體驗達悟族特有文化、欣賞自然生態、品味飛魚美食、欣賞拼板舟、享受海裡浮潛；如果時間剛好，還可以見識到達悟族人出海捕飛魚的景象。當然，造訪部落時更不能錯過達悟族豐富的祭儀活動，像是三月到六月的飛魚季節；八到九月雕舟下海禮及家屋落成禮等等。心動想要行動之前，最好先確定時間及地點。

洽詢電話：

- 台東縣政府　電話：089-326141　網址http://www.taitung.gov.tw/
- 蘭嶼鄉公所民政科　電話：089-732112

達悟族
文化導覽圖

族語開口說　　**入境隨俗的達悟語**

你好！
akokay!
阿姑蓋

你好！
akokay!
阿姑蓋

我的名字叫希南‧巴娜妲燕。
ngaran ko am　Sinan Panatayan.
阿然　　姑 阿門 希南　巴娜妲燕
（註:達悟族人都先自我介紹是誰，才請問對方是誰。）

請問貴姓？
sino ngaran mo?
西奴 阿然　　目

請問你住哪裡？
do jino yamo pey vahayan?
杜 吉奴 亞母 背　發阿晏

我家住在東清部落。
komey vahay doji ranmeylek.
姑米　　發霞 杜吉 然美樂可

這是什麼？
ikongo oya?
一姑奴 烏亞

這是達悟族的飛魚。
oya ranam alibangbang no tao.
烏亞 然阿門 阿立棒棒　　奴 達悟

你們中午吃些什麼？
ikongo o yanyo kanen no yamararaw?
一姑奴 烏 亞紐　嘎嫩　奴 亞馬然如

我們吃地瓜和飛魚。
namen koman so wakey a kano alibangbang.
那們　　姑曼　書 挖蓋 阿 嘎奴 阿立棒棒

你們要去那裡？
kanniw mangey do anjin?
嘎安　馬愛　杜 安吉

我們正預備招飛魚的祭品。
namen mi sinmosinmo so yabi rayon
那門　米 帝母帝母　書 亞比 然又安

我真的很喜歡你們的部落。
yako i　kakza o ili　niw.
亞姑 一 嘎拉 烏 一立 紐

感謝你來到我的島。
ayoy　do moni pakaranes　do pongso namen.
阿又一 杜 母尼 巴嘎然尼絲 杜 碰書　那門

那麼我回去了。
mangey ko ranan.
馬愛　姑 然那安

祝一路順風。
maka piyo ka so kataotao　an.
馬嘎 比亞 嘎 書 嘎大烏大烏 阿安

族語開口說　達悟族稱謂的介紹

ama	阿馬	爸爸
ina	伊娜	媽媽
akey	阿蓋	阿公
akes	阿絲	阿媽
maran	馬然	伯伯、叔叔、舅舅
kaminan	嘎米那安	阿姨或姑姑
kaka	嘎嘎	哥哥或姊姊
wari	娃熱	弟弟或妹妹

學習加油站　本書漢語與達悟語名詞對照表

故事01：竹生人和石生人

用漢字拼讀	達悟語	漢語名詞
嘎然姑萬 奴 娃娃	karakowan no wawa	太平洋
碰樹	pongso	島嶼
阿夢	among	魚
姑姑路	gogolo	貝殼
嘎又	kayo	樹木
阿比雅	apiya	美麗
大麼可 或 姑就浪	tamek 或 kochozang	蘭花
夫尼旦	vonitan	百合花
俄什門 奴 姑讓	esem no korang	山菊花
巴阿巴愛的	pahabahad	珠光鳳蝶
夫的大可 或 巴安笨	votdak 或 panganpen	白鼻心
杜杜霧	totowo	角鴞
娃襪	wawa	海
媽巴羊呀拉可	mapangyangyalak	古怪
媽大又	mataya	神秘
大大臘	tatala	船
阿放	avang	非達悟族人製作的其他船
達悟	tao	人
巴告	pakow	肩膀
媽大	mata	眼睛
力罵	lima	手掌
阿益	ai	腳
希·亞蓋 大杜 肚	Si-yakay do to	神
阿尼杜	anito	鬼
媽安尼可	mamnek	特殊能力
希·巴雷	Si-paloy	人名
希·烏拉曼	Si-ozamen	人名
嘎然達晏	karatayan	陸地
米木挖木挖／阿民阿姑	mimowamowa / amhako	耕種
媽阿阿阿波	mangahahap	捕魚
希·蓋雷提	Si-kaleted	人名
阿尼的	anit	天空
媽嘎讓	makarang	高
媽娥娥伯	mahephep	矮

用漢字拼讀	達悟語	漢語名詞
希・杷吉拉勞	Si-pacilalaw	人名
媽大法	matava	胖
嘎娜幹	kanakan	小孩
媽露肚以	malotoy	懷孕
媽發各絲	mevakes	婦女
姑曼	koman	吃
拉比可	lapik	鳥
媽沙愛	masaray	快樂
米亞努阿奴問的	miyanowanowod	歌唱
達悟 杜 嘎嘎然岸	tao do kakarangan	天上的人
米可尼伯	mikehnep	洪水
然奴門	ranom	水
伊然待	Iratay	漁人部落
然姑 阿 發杜	rako a vato	大石頭
伊木入的	Imowrod	紅頭部落
嘎娃爛 或 嘎畏	kawalan 或 kawoy	竹子
阿米安 杜 發愛	amyan do vahey	生小孩
烏呀的	oyat	神力
麼阿蓋	mehakey	男
媽發各絲	mevakes	女
伊立	ili	部落
米辛 目	misin mo	結婚
嘎大烏大烏	kataotao	身體
媽媽細了	mamasil	釣魚
媽吉發愛發愛	macivahvahey	嫁
媽巴拉可比特	mapazakpit	娶
媽的能	mateneng	聰明
阿比雅 書 嘎大烏大烏	apiya so kataotao	健康
的呢的能	teneteneng	智慧、知識
媽那巴沙巴 書 巴熱安	manapasapa so parngen	技藝
阿布	apow	子孫
挖蓋	wakey	地瓜
書書立	sosoli	芋頭
阿米立大　媽嘎嘎待	amlida makakadey	植物
都米奴問	tominon	織布
阿門阿姑	amhakow	開墾
阿沙嘎發愛	asakavahey	家人

用漢字拼讀	達悟語	漢語名詞
阿沙 書 伊那萬	asa so inawan	族人
尼 媽阿媽五可 阿 達悟	ni mangamawog a tao	造物者
碰書 奴 達悟	bongso no tao	人所居住的島嶼

故事02：飛魚之神

用漢字拼讀	達悟語	漢語名詞
伊那布	inapo	祖先
嘎嫩	kanen	食物
阿立棒棒	alibangbang	飛魚
書媽拉巴	somalap	飛翔
米了拉可 立棒棒	mizezyaka libangbang	飛魚之神
阿路	azo	禮物
媽西阿特	masingat	尊貴
大對呢伯	tateynep	夢
嘎曼熱熱各	kamanrarakeh	長老
媽阿熱路	mangarilow	愛
媽希嘎尼可	masikanig	尊重
米然又安	mirayon	飛魚季和飛魚祭的說法相同
拉拉萬	zazawan	飛魚架
媽奴罵	mangoma	豐收
米尹沙可	miisak	海流
米大襪了 書 立棒棒	mitawaz so libangbang	捕飛魚
的人尼	teyngi	陸蟹
阿旦 阿 立棒棒	adan a libangbang	飛魚乾
阿比雅	apiya	吉祥
馬阿廢	mangavey	罵人
媽嘎那門	maganam	跳舞
讓讓各	rarakeh	老人
然俄	rahet	男人吃的魚
盎沙阿	angsa	老人吃的魚
烏悠的	oyod	女人吃的魚
伊熱愛熱愛晏	ireyrayan	臥房
巴那的案	panadngan	靠背石
嘎達悟達悟	kataotao	自己
烏奴呢的	onowned	心

故事03：達悟拼板舟

用漢字拼讀	達悟語	漢語名詞
嘎讓門	karam	老鼠
達悟 杜 對熱阿門	tao do teyrahem	地底人
米大大臟	mitatala	造船
都了阿安 奴 讓奴門	tozngan no ranom	水洞
杜伊立那門	do ili namen	家鄉
曼拉沙 書 嘎又	manzasa so kayo	伐木
亞都那伊俄仍	yatonaingehreng	聲音
讓讓可	rarakeh	年長
亞比雅 書 伊亞俄	apiya so iyagey	友善
馬讓讓等	mararaten	自私
比讓讓拉萬	piraralawan	破壞
阿拉路	alalow	災難
伊那阿阿辦	inahahapan	漁獲
媽吉發發俄絲	macivahvahes	適量
嘎拉達宴	karatayan	土地
巴媽熱安	pamaringan	祭典
巴路絲	pazos	祭品
亞南 杜 立大南	yanan do lidanan	環境
阿撥拉旦	apzatan	保護
嘎阿山	kahasan	山林
麼尼	mehni	堅固
媽拉昂	maznga	笑
杜妹嘎待	tomeykaday	大自然
吉 妹立目瞪	ji meylimoteng	神聖
木亞的	mowyat	勤勞
烏飛	ovi	山藥
嘎大易	kadai	小米
大麼可	tamek	雜草
姑易絲	kois	豬
嘎可令	kaglin	羊
媽甘紐	makannyow	禁忌
亞米 給特地的安	yami keyteytetngehan	成員
米發賴	mivazey	工作
米發飛扇	mivavehsan	悼念
亞媽巴路娃絲	yamapalwas	下水儀式
讓辣	rala	血
媽媽能 書 嘎嫩	mamarem so kanen	祭船
媽西巴阿熱路	masipangarilow	分享

用漢字拼讀	達悟語	漢語名詞
他他拉 奴 達悟	tatala no tao	拼板舟
伊娃娃拉門	iwawawlam	生活
伊吉吉讓娃特	icicirawat	文化

故事04：林投樹下的男孩

用漢字拼讀	達悟語	漢語名詞
嘎發發大呢恩	kavavatanen	故事
媽拉發又	malavayo	年輕
媽安那黑	mannyahey	害怕
媽入	marow	白天
媽俄伯	mahep	夜晚
達悟語用漢字拼讀	達悟語	漢語名詞
發樂可	velek	肚子
哥給	kekey	嬰兒
阿奴	ango	林投樹
米亞分杜發愛	miyaven do vahey	夫妻
媽拉門	malam	走
阿米立恩	amizngen	聽
阿門拉飛	amlavi	哭
米亞嫩伯可	miyanenbek	刺
媽發可絲	mavakes	妻子
吉安娃特	cinwat	開水
發文 奴 嘎那甘	vawon no kanakan	母奶
米亞拉拉門	miyalalam	玩
書目立	somozi	氣憤
阿比亞書伊亞嘿	apiya so iyangey	溫柔
阿那可 阿 媽阿蓋	anak a mahakey	兒子
馬嘎飛付	maka veyvow	成熟
嘎路阿路夫旦	kaloowalovotan	社會
立布絲	zipos	親友
馬路矣	mazoway	光榮
馬阿熱路 書 那布萬	mangarilo so nyapowan	孝敬
阿拉路夫萬 那 阿那可	azwazovowon na anak	養育
阿比亞 飛安	apiya vehan	吉祥的日子
阿又引	ayoin	感恩
飛尼	viniy	肉

挑戰 Q&A

信心滿滿，阿美、卑南、達悟族
大小事輕鬆答！

▶ 阿美族

1. 在阿美族人心目中，福通是個發明家，請問他用了什麼新奇的玩意，轉眼間就將荒地變良田？

2. 莎樣雖然懷孕在身，仍然十分堅持陪福通回到天上的家，最後莎樣和福通是否順利的爬上天梯回家了？天梯放在現在的什麼地方？

3. 芝希麗薾長得非常漂亮，海神對她一見鍾情，請問海神用了什麼方法要脅懷露法絲將女兒嫁給祂？

4. 芝希麗薾的母親懷露法絲帶著一根鐵手杖，鐵手杖施展了什麼神奇法力？

5. 巨人阿里嘎該可以自由變幻人形，他曾變成哪些人的模樣，打亂阿美族人的生活？

6. 傳說中，巨人阿里嘎該住在哪一座山？這座山又坐落在現在的何處？

7. 阿美族勇士隊能夠有驚無險的打敗巨人阿里嘎該，多虧勇士隊領袖卡浪夢見什麼人告訴他方法？

8. 馬糾糾漂流到一個陌生的地方，眼前所見都是女人，沒有任何男人，傳說中女人國的女人如何生小孩？

9. 「螃蟹人的秘密」這則傳說故事，看完後有什麼心得？

▶ 卑南族

1. 卑南族南王部落人心目中的聖山是哪一座山？

2. 聖山又被稱為什麼山？這座山位在哪一縣市？

3. 卑南語中「會所」怎麼說？會所又扮演著什麼樣的功能？

4. 「普悠瑪」可以是卑南族名，也可以用來稱呼南王部落；在卑南語中，「普悠瑪」又代表什麼深遠的意思？

5. 奧馬樣用了什麼方法將弟弟依布萬救出來？依布萬逃出來之後，隨手拋下刀子又發生了什麼事？

6. 外祖母妲達姥教奧那樣和依布萬哪些報仇的方法？最後，發生了什麼事？

7. 卑南族南王部落人為什麼將「達拉拉不灣」視為禁地？卑南語中「達拉拉不灣」又是什麼意思？

8. 感恩海祭只有在哪個部落中舉行？海祭會在哪三個地方面向哪裡祭獻？

9. 德馬拉紹找到了可以當做主食的植物，究竟是什麼植物？最後，他是怎麼帶回給族人的？

10. 巴塔吉烏為什麼被族人放逐到海外的小島？徬徨無助的巴塔吉烏又是如何回到家中？

11. 這些發生在台灣遠古時代的神話與傳說故事，看完之後有什麼心得？

▶ 達悟族

1. 蘭嶼位在台灣的哪個方向？試著畫出兩島的位置關係圖。

2. 美麗的蘭嶼島上蘊藏珍貴又稀有的動植物，你可以舉出三種嗎？

3. 天上的人派了哪兩個孩子，讓達悟族人可以繼續繁衍後代？你知道祂們將蘭嶼島叫做什麼？

4. 飛魚之神叮嚀達悟族人只能在適當的季節捕捉飛魚，而且只要取足夠的量就好了，想想看原因是什麼？

5. 如果要在飛魚季節造訪蘭嶼，最好哪幾個月去？你知道過去達悟族人利用什麼方法，吸引飛魚群跳上船？

6. 達悟族人擁有獨一無二的造船技巧，傳說中是誰傳授給他們的？

7. 達悟族人造出來的船隻，堅固、耐用又美麗，請問他們造出來的船叫做什麼？

8. 達悟族是男女分工的社會，你知道男人和女人各負責什麼工作嗎？

9. 新船下水前要舉行下水儀式，船身將會堆滿水芋、地瓜，你知道這是為什麼？

10. 被拋棄在林投樹下的男孩，得知自己身世之後，用什麼方式來回報親生母親和扶養他的老夫婦？

E網情報站

輕鬆上網搜尋,「原味」超靈通

這些團體默默耕耘,收集整理了有關原住民文化、原鄉風光等等豐富內容,趕快上網共享!

1 **蘭嶼鄉公所**

　提供蘭嶼最新新聞、自然生態、傳統住屋、歲時祭儀、部落傳說,以及豐富的觀光旅遊資訊。

2 **中央研究院・蘭嶼專題**

　由中研院各所共同合作的虛擬博物館,館藏豐富,其中的「蘭嶼專題」包含蘭嶼人文社會及自然生態研究資料。

3 **國立台灣史前文化博物館**

　以保存、研究卑南等重要遺址及其出土古文物的文化遺留為主,展示並致力推廣考古學、人類學等社會文化教育。

4 **台東縣政府全球資訊網**

　詳細介紹台東縣的地理環境及人文歷史、光觀景點,並提供全年度的文化光觀資訊,只要點選「觀光行事曆」,台東旅遊資訊隨時掌握。

5 **交通部觀光局花東縱谷國家風景管理處**

　一次飽覽台灣花東縱谷的綺麗風光及人文特色,並可了解當地的光觀資源、遊憩據點、旅遊資訊,還有貼心的行程安排建議等資訊。

6 **行政院原住民族委員會/原住民資訊網**

　舉凡原住民權益、法規、族群及文化介紹等等,十分豐富。

7 **原住民族委員會原住民族文化發展中心**

　有原住民園區風采介紹、山海的精靈(原住民介紹)、原鄉藝文、兒童園地、母語教室等,相當值得流覽。

8 **台北市政府原住民族事務委員會**

　介紹台灣原住民各族群,並呈現歷年來台北原住民文化祭活動內容。

9　順益台灣原住民博物館

順益台灣原住民博物館為人類學博物館，館內主要蒐藏、研究並展示台灣原住民文物，藉教育活動的推廣，呈現台灣本土文化多樣面貌。

10　九族文化村－原住民文化

網頁中有原住民文化介紹、部落景觀、歷史照片、音樂，以及傳統手工藝的概述。

11　原舞者

原住民藉由歌曲及舞蹈將傳統文化、歷史代代相傳，因此「原舞者」致力於將原住民歌舞藝術推廣傳承，更希望走向世界。

12　山海文化雜誌社

以維護並發展原住民文化、促進社會對原住民的了解與尊重為宗旨；網站提供協會簡介與消息、山海出版社出版資訊。

13　公共電視原住民新聞雜誌

提供有關原住民新聞、活動訊息、原住民資料庫。

14　幸福綠光股份有限公司

【台灣原住民的神話與傳說】透過生動的故事，搭配精緻彩繪圖畫，勾勒出原住民信仰、儀式、禁忌、圖騰、生活智慧與技能，並透過中、英文對照，希望讓國人以及海外讀者能認識台灣原住民寶貴的生活文化遺產，也讓台灣這段遠古歷史變得清晰、鮮活、可親。

15　花蓮縣原住民民族教育資源中心

花蓮縣設立原住民民族教育資源中心，積極研發、推廣原住民民族課程和教學，蒐集及整理文物資訊，協助並支援原住民民族教學活動。

16　南王Puyuma花環實小

點選「鄉土教學」有豐富的卑南族傳統文化導覽，在「普悠瑪部落」中可了解祭典、會所等訊息，也有猴祭、大狩獵祭的精采介紹。

阿美族
A　m　i　s

01

Votong's Fantastic Top

> A huge top was hurled into the air. Before long the spinning top had loosened the earth so the *Amis* could plant crops. They knew that *Votong*, the inventor of this marvelous top, was no ordinary person. From *Votong* the *Amis* learned the ways of cultivation, ceremony, and social custom. These customs and traditions were passed down from generation to generation.

A very long time ago there was a young couple, who according to legend, came out of the ground at the place known as *Nararacanan*. The man's name was *Votoc* and the woman's name was *Savak*.

Before long *Votoc* and *Savak* gave birth to a child they named *Votong*.

At this time there was also a woman by the name of *Kurumi* who lived with her daughter *Sayan*. No one knows from where they came, and all we can say is that they are the ancestors of the *Sakizaya* group of the *Amis* Tribe.

One morning Sayan carried an *atoma* to fetch water at the **tfon** in her usual manner. But when she tried to bring up the water, for some reason the rope was stuck and wouldn't budge.

Unable to get the water, she returned home and described the strange event to her mother. *Kurumi* told *Sayan* to return to the *tfon* and try again. When she got back and was about to try to fetch the water, a young man suddenly appeared, climbing out of the *tfon*. This young man was none other than *Votong*!

Votong was immediately very taken with *Sayan* and asked her to marry him. Although deep in her heart *Sayan* also liked *Votong* very much, she could not lightly agree to such an important matter as marriage without first obtaining her mother's consent. Thus, she took *Votong* home to meet her mother. When they arrived *Sayan* told her mother about the events at the well.

Kurumi thought *Votong* was quite nice looking and she could also see how much he cared for her daughter. She agreed to the marriage.

After *Votong* and *Sayan* married they lived with *Kurumi*. However, much to the dismay of those around them, *Votong*, did not like to work in the way that others worked. Rather, all day he stayed around the house making *'acocol*.

Kurumi was very unhappy about this and tried all kinds of ways to get *Votong* out of the house. *Kurumi* even had her neighbors and family put pressure on *Votong*, but all of their efforts failed to stir *Votong*.

One day after *Votong* had finished making a top, he went out to a wild area overgrown with all manner of tangled plants, trees, shrubs and brush. He took his top and spun it into the air with all his might. The top swirled and twirled, bouncing

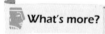

What's more?

Votong: in the minds of the *Amis Votong* was a brilliant inventor. Some stories credit him with having invented agricultural techniques while others say he invented fishing implements and the ladder. *Amis* will often refer to an intelligent person as *Votong* or *Wawa ni Votong* (son of Votong).

Nararacanan: the birth place of the Amis is located in the area of the present day Hualian Harbor, however with all the buildings and harbor machinery it is impossible to distinguish any historical vestiges.

Amis: the *Amis* of Hualian, generally north of Chihshang and Luyeh Townships refer to themselves as *Pangcah* which means "person." According to scholars the word "*Amis*" was borrowed from the *Puyuama* language and means "those from the north". There is still debate over the correct name for the tribe.

and spinning over the land. The top transformed the land into a field that was excellent for planting.

Votong then planted two melons, one sweet and one bitter. Rice grew from where the sweet melon had been planted and millet from the place of the bitter melon. Everyone was spellbound by his actions.

Later, *Votong* taught the people how to sow and plant, how to perform ritual, what activities should be *taboo* and what should be encouraged. Everyone now realized that *Votong* was no ordinary person. He had the gifts and powers of a spirit, and thereafter no one dared interfere with or criticize anything he did.

After three years *Votong* told *Sayan* that he longed to return to the land of his parents. Because, the trip would be such a long and strenuous one, he tried to persuade *Sayan* to stay behind.

However, *Sayan*, who was already pregnant, insisted on accompanying *Votong* on his journey home.

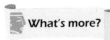
What's more?

Sakizaya: These people were included as part of the Amis until they were recognized as a discreet tribe in 2007. Mostly living around what is now Hualian City as a result of battles with Qing Chinese forces. Their language and the *Amis* language are mutually unintelligible.

atoma: Generally the *Amis* used bamboo implements to scoop up the water and stored the water in ceramic containers which the women would often be seen balancing on their heads. The *Amis* made pottery beginning a long time ago and today one can still see their traditional pottery in places such as *vata'an* (Matai'an).

tfon: the source from which *Sayan* was going to collect water is referred to by the *Amis* as *tfon-no-Votong*, or *Votong*'s well. Another version of the story calls this "*Votong*'s fishing spot". The historical area was filled in when building the airport in Hualian. Only a small pond in front of the Hualian Teachers College remains where people can pay tribute.

Votong's parents lived in the heavens. Near the end of the trip they would have to climb a ladder high into the sky. After traveling for a long time, *Votong* and *Sayan* finally arrived at the ladder.

Just as they were about to begin the climb, *Votong* instructed *Sayan* to be careful. He said, "While on the ladder you must not speak or make any sound at all". *Sayan* acknowledged and vowed to follow his guidance.

Step by step *Votong* and *Sayan* carefully ascended the ladder. They were but a few rungs away from the end, just about to enter the heavens. Suddenly, *Sayan*, who was thoroughly exhausted, let out a sigh, "Ahhhh".

Immediately the heavens seemed to collapse around them as the ladder twisted and turned in all sorts of contortions. *Sayan* was thrown to the ground below. As she lay dead far below, wild deer, mountain boar and snakes emerged from her belly. It was from this day that all the varied species of animals came into this world.

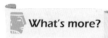 **What's more?**

masunanam: according to early records when a man and woman intended to marry, the engagement would be concluded when the man gave his neck jewelry to the woman, and the woman gave her head scarf to the man. If the engagement was to be ended, they would simply return the gifts.

pataloma': as *Amis* are a matriarchal society, marriage is centered around the woman. On the morning of the wedding the groom carries a jug of clear water on his head to his home to demonstrate gratitude, and then he takes a bundle of firewood to the woman's home as a symbol of perpetuation. The wedding takes place at the bride's home and here parents present the couple with two gifts: a machete for clearing brush on the mountain trails, and a lovers' bag which symbolizes that they are now a family. The bride gives the groom a betel nut to show her everlasting love and fidelity.

'acocol: the tops games played by the *Amis* were similar to those of the Han Chinese. They both would use twine to spin the tops, the tops would collide with one another, and the objective was to be the last one standing.

salsin: stories passed down have it that the *Sakizaya* performed millet sowing rituals that lasted for seven days, but with the introduction of rice this custom gradually disappeared.

Votong was unable to do anything to save *Sayan* as she plummeted to her death. Heartbroken, he returned home alone. Today, remnants of the ladder that he and *Sayan* climbed can still be seen in the Rui Hui Township of Hualien County.

Where did it come from?
This story was collected from the Sakol community (Guofu District in Hualian City).

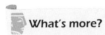

What's more?

taboo: taking the seven day millet sowing ritual of the *Sakizaya* as an example, on the third day it was prohibited to eat vegetables and white meat (e.g., chicken, fish), no bathing or hand washing was permitted on the fourth and fifth days for fear of washing away the soils that held the shoots of plants, and from the first to the fifth day, men and women were to abstain from sex so as not to offend the gods.

puyapuy: pregnant women were not to eat betel nuts or bananas that had grown in pairs as the *Amis* believed that giving birth to twins was inauspicious. The following were also taboo: no disrespect toward elders, no lying or scolding, no promiscuity, no taking of life, no contact with the dead. These proscriptions applied to all in the tribe, but it was believed that pregnant women should pay special attention lest they have a miscarriage.

Deer, boar, snakes: there are other versions of the story that have snakes, crocodiles and tortoises, emerging from Sayan's belly which is to say this was the origin of reptiles.

Sapad: *Amis* call the area where *Votong* and *Sayan* climbed the ladder, the *Sapad* stone pillars, which is known as the Wuhe terrace in the vicinity of Maibu/Maifor village. There are two stone pillars (originally three) in this important archaeological site in the East Rift Valley connecting Hualian and Taitung counties.

Vay-Rovas and Kafit the Sea Spirit

Cisiringan was so beautiful that she attracted even the attentions of *Kafit*, the sea sprit. *Kafit* was so moved by her beauty that he demanded that she be his wife. He threatened that unless the Amis agreed to turn her over to him he would bring floods to all of their lands. *Cisiringan*'s mother, *Vay-Rovas*, could not accept having her dear daughter taken from her like this. Walking stick in hand, she set out to the south to find *Kafit* and her stolen daughter.

We have heard the story of *Votong* and his magical top. In addition to *Votong*, *Votoc* and *Sayak* had a daughter *Vay-Rovas*.

Vay-Rovas bore a daughter by the name *Cisiringan*. *Cisiringan* grew up to be a great beauty. Her entire body emanated a soft red glow.

One day *Cisiringan* was playing by the sea when she was spotted by *Kafit*, the sea spirit. *Kafit* was so attracted by her beauty that he decided *Cisiringan* should become his wife.

Kafit said to *Cisiringan*'s mother that if she did not let him marry her daughter he would cause the waters to rise and flood their village.

Vay-Rovas had no intent to give up her daughter. She ignored *Kafit's* threats.

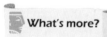

What's more?

Kafit: This sea spirit is the object of southern *Amis* ritual.

True to his word however, *Kafit* caused the water around the village rise higher and higher. All the *Nararacanan* villagers were worried about the flooding. They pleaded with *Vay-Rovas* to change her mind. They asked her to let *Kafit* to marry her daughter so their village could be saved.

Vay-Rovas could not bear the thought of losing her daughter, but finally she had no choice.

Vay-Rovas put *Cisiringan* in a large basket and set her adrift on the ocean. All of a sudden the sea turned a shade of red, and then the waters gradually began to recede. *Cisiringan* was nowhere to be seen.

After the waters receded, *Vay-Rovas* took an iron bar as a walking stick and set off in the direction where her daughter was last seen. Day and night she continued south along the shores of the ocean. She finally came to *Tarawadaw* but found no trace of her daughter.

Vay-Rovas was so sad that she threw down her walking stick and returned all alone to the *Nararacanan* village.

Vay-Rovas performed many feats of magic during her travels. She used her iron bar to split the land and the water so that she could pass. It is said that this is how the shapes of water and land came to be.

Where did it come from?

This story was collected from the Sakol community (Guofu District in Hualian City).

What's more?

Tarawadaw: located in the vicinity of the Hsiugulan River coastal estuary in Hualian.

karam: in traditional *Amis* society only the *cikawasay* or priest, is able to perform magic.

Alikakay the Giant Child Eater

Alikakay was a giant who's size terrified the Amis. He also had magic power and liked to cast harmful spells on the Amis. The Amis formed a group of warriors guided by Kafit, the Sea Spirit to do battle with and ultimately vanquish Alikakay.

Every year the Amis perform a ceremony to show their gratitude to Kafit for help in defeating *Alikakay*. The Amis' rigorous physical training for their young people is also a way of honoring *Kafit*.

Long ago on *Pazik* Mountain lived a giant. The nearby *Amis* villagers called the giant *Alikakay*.

Alikakay could perform all kinds of magic. He would often transform himself into a person and go among the *Amis* creating mischief. Things often became quite dangerous because of his antics.

Alikakay particularly liked to eat the internal organs of young children.

A young mother in the village had two daughters, one eight years old, and the other just an infant. The elder child was able to help her mother so one day when the young mother went to the fields with her daughters to work, she asked the elder daughter to take care of her younger sister. The older sister hoisted her infant sister on her back and joined their mother in the fields.

What's more?

Pazik: this is Meilun Mountain in present day Hualian City.

At noon as the mother was preparing to suckle her baby daughter, the elder sister thought something was strange and asked her mother: "Didn't you just feed baby sister? Why are you feeding her again so soon?"

Hearing this the mother also sensed that something was wrong. She hastened to examine her baby, and to her shock she found the infant was already dead with all her internal organs cleanly eaten away. All that remained was a clump of straw in her stomach. *Alikakay* had changed into the likeness of her mother and when elder sister thought the infant was being cared for, *Alikakay* was eating the child's organs!

Another strange incident involved a family of the same village. One day the husband went out fishing as usual. The wife stayed at home doing her chores with the children awaiting the husband's return. However, on that particular day the husband showed up much earlier than usual carrying an enormous basket filled with all kinds of fish.

The whole family feasted on the delicious fish after which the husband and wife went to bed. They had not been sleeping long when the wife was suddenly awakened by a loud knock at their door. When she opened the door she saw none other than her husband standing in front of her! There was no one in her bed!

They then realised that this was *Alikakay* playing tricks on them.

These sorts of strange and terrible incidents occurred so often that the Amis lived in constant fear of *Alikakay*.

The *mato'asay* gathered together to discuss what they should do. How could they prevent these things from happening? They decided that all the children of the village would be gathered together in the *talu'an*, and there they would be guarded and taken care of by the village youth. Women were never to be left alone, whether they were at home or outside. For a short time these measures were enough to keep *Alikakay* away.

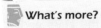 **What's more?**

mitafukud: Amis are very adept fishers with most using the octangonal net and some using fixed nets or spears.

futing: the Amis do not reserve specific fish for specific persons.

However, these measures could not stop *Alikakay* for long. *Alikakay* was especially hungry, not having eaten for some time. One day he went to the *talu'an*, reached through the roof and tried to grab one of the children inside for his next meal. However, the children were being guarded by the youth who were well prepared for such an attack. Not only did *Alikaay* not get his meal, he lost an arm when it was chopped off by the young guards!

Alikakay retreated only a short distance. He went into the nearby mountains and used his magic to transform a tree trunk into a new arm.

The elders in the village decided that they must do something to get rid of *Alikakay* once and for all. *Pazik*, the *kakitaan*, assembled the elders and all of the village youth, divided them into groups based on their age, and then designated two warrior groups, the *Lalikit* and the *Likuda*.

During the one month before the two groups set out to find *Alikakay* they went through rigorous training in short and long distance sprinting, survival in the wilderness, and archery.

After completing their training, the two groups of warriors patiently awaited orders from the elders.

When the elders gave the order, the warriors set out to find and destroy *Alikakay*. They engaged him in battle at the site of *Pazik* Mountain. Although at first the warriors had the upper hand, it was not long before *Alikakay* began using his magic. The warriors were helpless and many were killed or seriously injured. All of the *Amis'* skill with fire and arrows was useless against *Alikakay*. They were unable to cause him the slightest harm.

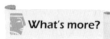 **What's more?**

talu'an is a gathering place for young men and is also the administrative, educational and military center of the community.

mato'asay: the elders of a village constitute the highest decision making body.

kakitaan: in traditional Amis society decisions are made by the chief and the elders and implemented by others according to their age group.

Lalikit, Likuda: these are now two dances of the Amis performed only during the annual harvest festival.

kapah: young people are recruited into a group of "braves".

Finally one of the leaders, *Kalang*, gave the order to retreat. *Kalang* was very upset about his warrior's defeat at the hands of *Alikakay*. He had let his people down. He was confused and had no idea of what he should do. One day he walked so far that he fell into a stupor. Thoroughly exhausted, he came upon a large stone, laid down and went to sleep.

In his deep sleep the voice of *Kafit*, the sea spirit came to him: "*Kalang*, victory against *Alikakay* is easy. Simply use the *Porong*, and you will be able to overpower his magic."

After *Kalang* awoke and told the elders about *Kafit*'s advice, they agreed to give it a try. All of the *Amis* began collecting *Porong* in preparation for the next battle with *Alikakay*.

On the day of the decisive battle *Kalang* ordered all of the warriors to wear the *Porong*. As predicted by *Kafit*, *Alikakay*'s magic could not stop the warriors who were wearing *Porong*. They easily and quickly defeated *Alikakay*.

Alikakay went to the sea, never to be seen again.

To this day, although the *Amis* lead peaceful lives, no one has forgotten the lessons of their training. Every year during the harvest festival, the training of youth is an important part of the village activities. At the same time, they honor *Kafit*, never forgetting how the sea spirit helped them in their time of need.

Where did it come from?
This story was collected from the Sakol community (Guofu District in Hualian City).

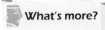

What's more?

Porong: a grass that is shaped into an arrow by using reeds to bind it's lower part together. It is often used as a ceremonial implement.

Milisin Mila'dis: while many of the traditions of indigenous peoples have become much less pronounced or have even disappeared as industrial society takes over, however the Harvest Festival, *Milison*, and the Sea Festival, *Mila'dis*, remain important annual events for the Amis.

04

Maciwciw's Visit to the Land Without Men

> After days of sleeping *Maciwciw* was startled to awaken and find himself surrounded by women! Even more shocking was that they planned to fatten him up and eat him! Luckily, a sympathetic young girl and a great whale helped him escape. After he returned home he went to the sea every year to pay tribute to the young woman and the great whale.

Long ago there was a young man named *Maciwciw*. Every day *Maciwciw* worked long and hard. One day when *Maciwciw* went to the fields to work as usual it began to rain heavily.

So much rain fell that the river rose over its banks. *Maciwciw* was caught in the violent currents and was carried off to the sea. But he managed to grab onto a piece of wood and save himself from drowning.

No one knows for how long *Maciwciw* bobbed about in the ocean before he came to an unknown island. The area looked familiar and was similar to his home, so he set out to find a settlement.

Maciwciw walked for a very long time with seeing any signs of people. He was very tired from all the walking so he laid down next to a tree to take a little nap. Just as he was nodding off, he thought he heard voices. There seemed to be the faint the sound of people coming toward him.

Suddenly, he found himself surrounded by people clutching knives and spears. All of these people were women!

A very beautiful woman among the group said: "What is this thing? I've never seen anything like it before! But it does look tasty!"

Maciwciw wanted to run away, but anticipating his escapte the women captors tied him up. They then took the terrified *Maciwciw* back to their village.

In the village there were no men. Everything was done by women.

These women gave birth in a very special way. When a woman wanted to have a child she simply went to a tall mountain near the village where she would greet the wind with open arms. As a gentle wind passed over her arms a child would be born, emerging from her armpit.

Because they could bear children on their own, no men were needed, and they had never even seen a man!

Maciwciw was kept in a large cage some distance away from the village. Not long after he had been in the cage a beautiful woman came to inspect the new arrival. This woman commanded great respect from all the others and *Maciwciw* thought that she must be the chief.

She carefully inspected *Maciwciw* and said: "This animal looks quite delicious! However, it is a little too lean, so let's fatten it up and it will surely be even tastier!" With that, she turned around and went back to her village.

The next day when it was time to eat, a young woman brought *Maciwciw* a feast with all kinds of delicacies. However, *Maciwciw* didn't dare eat too much because he remembered what the chief had said about fattening him up. He was afraid that as soon as he gained weight he would be killed and eaten.

Although he tried to escape, the cage was too strong. Unable to break out, he waited out the days patiently, never eating too much. After a while *Maciwciw* noticed that the same woman brought him his food every day. She seemed nice and to have a good heart. *Maciwciw* decided to ask her for help.

One day when the young woman brought his food at the usual time *Maciwciw* asked for her help.

Not having heard him speak before, the young woman was startled. But now she knew *Maciwciw* was human, and so she agreed to help him.

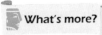

What's more?

kakitaan: the Amis' leaders or chiefs are not restricted based on gender.

She stayed with him while he ate and then before returning to her village, the young woman handed *Maciwciw* her knife. That evening *Maciwciw* used the knife to break out of his cage. Once out of the cage he took off in a run toward the sea.

But someone had discovered his escape. By the time he got to the shores of the sea many women carrying satotom were in pursuit. He was terrified of what they would do if they caught up to him, and had no idea of how he could get to safety.

As he was standing on the seashore a great whale suddenly came by and said to Maciwciw: "I am a friend of the young woman who helped you escape. I have come here to take you home".

Just as the women in pursuit were closing in *Maciwciw* jumped on to the whale's back. The whale sped out to sea, chased by women throwing spears. Some even tried to follow in boats but they were not fast enough to catch the whale. *Maciwciw* had escaped the fate of being the main course of a feast!

The great whale swam to *Maciwciw*'s home. No sooner had he climbed off the whale than it was gone. *Maciwciw* didn't even have time to thank the whale.

Upon arriving in his village, no one recognized him. *Maciwciw* had been away for so many years! To show his gratitude to the young women and the great whale, every year *Maciwiciw* went to the sea shore and laid out 'icep, torom and 'epah as offerings. This ritual is the origin of one of the Amis Sea Festivals.

Where did it come from?

This story was collected from the Sakol community (Guofu District in Hualian City).

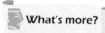

What's more?

satotom: to fashion torches for lighting, Amis would tightly bind straw.

torom: a kind of cake made from glutinous rice.

'epah: it is said that in the early days 'epah, or beverage alchohol was made from saliva and millet by the purest young woman in the village.

'icep: peoples that place great importance on the betel nut include the *Amis*, *Puyuma*, *Paiwan*, and *Rukai*. The use of betel nuts by other peoples came later. For the Amis the betel nut is an essential part of many rituals and is also important when making friends.

05

Story of the Crabman

> Never before had anyone seen such a person. He was no larger than a child, and had the head of a human but the body of a crab. Not only did His parents not abandon him, they helped him to find a wife! One day the "Crabman" suddenly transformed into a tall and handsome man. The family always gave thanks to the spirits for giving them a normal life, and to this day the special genes have been carried down from generation to generation of the Amis.

On the east coast of Taiwan there once lived an *Amis* couple who made their living from fishing and collecting mollusks. They gave birth to a child that grew up to be quite unlike any child they had ever seen: he had the head of a human but the body of a crab.

At first they were going to throw the child into the sea and let it fend for itself. However, they couldn't bear the thought of doing this. After all, it was their own child, no matter what it looked like.

One day when the infant was not yet even a year old he suddenly began speaking to his parents: "Thank you mother and father for not abandoning me. You will see that someday I will become a person just like everyone else. Although the parents could hardly believe their ears, they resolved to take special care of this special "Crabman" child.

The Crabman didn't eat very much, and when he slept he used *papah no pawli* as a blanket. He would sometimes help his parents with tasks such as collecting firewood along the seashore.

One day, the Crabman said to his parents that he wanted to get married and asked them to help him find a wife. His parents had no idea what to do. They said to him:

"It is not that we don't want to help you, but we are afraid that we won't be able to find anyone willing to marry you!"

The Crabman was not put off by this and he kept on asking his parents to help find him a wife. Having no other choice, the parents hopefully set out to the neighboring villages in search of a willing woman for their son.

After searching far and wide, they finally found someone. They didn't tell her about their son's appearance, and they didn't allow her to see her husband after the two were married.

One day, having became so impatient, she complained to Crabman's parents: "I have already been married for a long time. I have done nothing wrong, yet why do you not let me see my husband?"

The young woman announced her intention to leave them and began her preparations. The Crabman's worried parents discussed the matter with their son.

The Crabman told his parents: "Last night I had a dream that I had become a normal person. You must wrap me in *papah no pawli* and place me in the wooden bucket at the well. No matter what, you must keep my wife here for one more night."

After the parents had listened to their son's plan, they said to their daughter in law: "If you really want to leave, we can't stop you. So please just wait for a little while ; we can go to the mountains and gather some treats for you to take back with you." She was thus persuaded to stay for one more day.

The next morning when the young girl went to the well to fetch water to wash her face, she discovered a very peculiar child in the water bucket. But when the morning sun shone on the child, he suddenly grew into a handsome young man.

The Crabman told the young woman the whole story of his life. After she recovered from her shock, she realized that the Crabman was actually her own husband

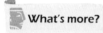

What's more?

papah no pawli: in some villages in northern Hualian, papah no pawli, or banana leaves are fashioned into magical implements to facilitate spells and rituals.

and she then understood the reason why the Crabman's parents had not let her see her husband.

After a little while the Crabman and his wife gave birth to two children, a boy and a girl.

One day when the Crabman and his wife went out to work, they told their daughter to take care of her younger brother. The young girl dutifully agreed and she rocked her younger brother in his cradle. When he was soundly asleep she went out to play with the neighbor children.

A short time later she came back home to check up on her little brother. To her surprise a young man whom she had never seen before was standing in the doorway looking this way and that.

Before the strange man could say a word, the young girl blurted out a string of questions: "Who are you", "What are you doing here?". The man looked at her sincerely and said, "Miss, I am your younger brother! Perhaps you do not believe me, but you can test what I say: ask me something about your family that outsiders could never know."

The young girl dashed over to the basket, and was amazed to discover that her brother was gone.

She turned to the strange man and decided to question him as he had suggested. She was astonished to find that no matter what she asked about her family he knew all the answers.

Nevertheless, the young girl still had her doubts. Just then the Crab couple returned. When the young girl told them about her experience with the strange man her parents said: "That's right, he is your brother."

Thus was the Crab family very special. In each generation there was one child who grew up exceptionally fast.

Where did it come from?

This story was collected from the Sakol community (Guofu District in Hualian City).

卑南族
Puyuma

Stories from the Puyuma of Dulan Mountain

> A great flood covered the land of the Puyuma Tribe's Ancestors. They set out on the ocean in search of a new home. All humans share the desire to overcome adversity and to search for one's dreams.

It is said that Dulan Mountain (*Tuangalan*) is the original settlement of the Nanwang Puyuma.

Long, long ago, their ancestors lived faraway in an unknown land. Floods brought landslides and the disasters left the people with no means of survival.

 What's more?

Dulan Mountain is known to the Puyuma as *Tuangalan* or *maiDangan* reverential titles meaning "Mountain of the Elders" or "Mountain of the Ancestors".

Nanwang Village in 1930 while Taiwan was under the control of the Japanese government, Puyuma tribespeople living in the area of Nanwang were afflicted with a serious epidemic. For considerations of hygiene and relieving pressures of over-population the people were relocated west to a place known as *sakuban*, known today as *Nanwang Village*. Another small group of people moved to what is today Baosang Li in Taitung City. This group is called Nanwang sakuban, while the Nanwang people still like to use *puyuma* to indicate their lineage.

The male and female elders, *adulumaw* and *adulusaw*, assembled five or six families, altogether more than thirty members of the tribe. In their wooden boats they set out on the seas in search of a home.

Over the seas they traveled until they came to the island of *buTul* which is known today as Orchid Island. Although there were people already living on buTul the Puyuma nevertheless decided to settle here.

The customs of these island peoples were very different and frequent conflicts arose between the original residents and the newcomers. *adulumaw* and *adulusaw* decided that *buTul* was not a good place to settle, so they built new boats stocked with water and food to sustain them on their next journey. Once again, they set out again in search of their new and permanent home.

Upon departing from *buTul* they wandered aimlessly on the sea for many days with no land was in sight. The rolling motion of the ocean waves below and the dizzying heat of the bright sun overhead made everyone seasick. But despite their discomfort they were determined to go on until they found their own place to settle, a place they could call home.

One day, far off on the horizon they spotted land. It was in the shape of an upside-down cooking pot! All were excited and they used their last bits of energy to paddle towards the shore. Upon landing, they discovered a paradise with abundant plants and animals. Most suitable for settlement! This, according to their story was what is now known as Dulan Mountain.

After landing at Dulan Mountain, *adulumaw* grasped a handful of earth and threw it into the ocean. He called upon the ocean to recede its waters, and recede they did. *adulusaw* shouted out: "Women, now you have level ground to plant our crops."

The ancestors of the Nanwang villagers lived in the area of Dulan Mountain for several hundred years. The land was rich with food and the population naturally increased. They now had a new problem: what could they do when they had so many people but not enough land?

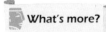

What's more?

buTul refers to present day Lanyu or Orchid Island.

At this time, one of the ancestors discovered a large plain at the foot of Dulan Mountain. The area was both large enough and had sufficient resources to support all of their people.

All of the members of the village discussed moving to this newly discovered area.

At first, seven brothers and sisters went to the area beneath Dulan Mountain. Each of them selected a suitable place to settle and build a home. Later, the word got out to the others who had stayed behind that these seven families were living quite well. The others then began to move to the plains. The seven locations of the original seven brothers and sisters became seven different hamlets and the other people chose their hamlets based on preference for the location, because of family ties, or for other reasons.

During their migration to the plains, some elders, upon arriving at a hot springs area called *apangan*, were so exhausted that they decided to stay behind. The elders settled here while the others continued their journey to the plains at the foot of Dulan Mountain.

Upon reaching the plains, the others began to worry about the elders left behind, so they sent young men and women back up the mountain to deliver food to their relatives living at *apangan*. They repeated this regularly and the practice become part of the *gemamul* performed each year during the *mangayaw* or Great Hunting Rites of the Nanwang village. These rites are still practiced today.

The peoples of the Beinan plains established several distinct hamlets and made their living by hunting and simple agriculture. Before going out to hunt however, they would strictly perform certain rituals. Among the most important of these rituals was the "bonding exercise" of the males in the group.

What's more?

Seven settlements: the seven villages of the Puyuma tradition are *mayDadar, babaTulan, arawaraway, kulkulungan, kanautu, mununung*, and *bukit*.

apangan: hot springs located near to present day Rongshan Village, Yanping Township, Taidong County.

mangayaw: among the major Puyuma festivals.

gemamul : Whirling Rice ceremonies.

At the hamlet of *maiDadar* the older brother built a structure known to them as a *palakuwan*. We can call this a "meeting place", but as we will see, it was much more than just a "place to meet". The other groups followed this practice and soon they all had their own *palakuwan*.

In *Puyuma* society the *palakuwan* is very important. It is a kind of "men's association", and its function in some ways resembles a military camp. Here in the *palakuwan*, the unmarried adult men gather in preparation to defend against their enemies. At the same time, the palakuwan serves as a kind of school where young men receive teachings and wisdom from their elders.

After many years the people of the seven hamlets began to realize that if they were too spread out and lived in different places they would be more vulnerable to their enemies. After much discussion they decided they could take better care of one another if they lived together. The different groups then moved to the location of the older brother's hamlet of *mayDadar*.

This event known among the tribes as *"puyuma"* which means coming together or solidarity. This word *puyuma* gradually became the name for the Nanwang Villagers and the term *Puyuma* became the name for the entire tribe during the Japanese colonial era.

Where did it come from?

This story is based on a narrative by Chen Kuang-rong, then chairperson of the Nanwang Community Development Association.

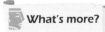 What's more?

mayDadar: one of the seven villages in the *Puyuma* tradition.

palakuwan: is sometimes called "man house" as it refers to a place where men gathered for various activities. It is also simply referred to as "meeting place".

The Mysterious Crescent Stones

During a period of great cataclysm the land of the *raranges* was all but destroyed by fire and earthquake. Only sheets of stone of unknown origin were left standing. These stones, which still stand upright between the land and the sky today in Taitung County, tell us and generations to come of this great natural upheaval.

Long, long ago there were two brothers of the *Puyuma*, *aunayan* the elder, and *ibuwan* the younger. In the middle of the night they liked to go out to the *aspan* fields planted by their neighbors, the *raranges*. In the fields they would trick the raranges by pretending to be *kuyu*, shouting out "jeee jeee, jeee jeee" to fool the *raranges*, and ate their fill of the sweet and fragrant sugar cane.

It didn't take long before some of the *raranges* discovered that it probably was not *kuyu* that were stealing into their *aspan* fields! They spread ashes all around the cane fields so that nothing could enter or leave without leaving tracks.

On the following day, sure enough, they found not tracks of *kuyu* but footprints of people! They now had clear evidence that people stealing from their fields.

That evening the raranges hid in waiting. The two brothers having no clue that the raranges were onto them, went into the fields as usual, shouting out their *kuyu* imitations. The *raranges* surrounded and tried to capture them.

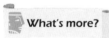 **What's more?**

raranges: it is still not known as to what tribe this name refers.

aspan: sugar cane.

kuyu: *Melogale moschata subaurantiaca* or Formosan Ferret Badger, is an endemic carnivorous mammal living at altitudes between sea level and approximately 2000 meters.

The taller of the two brothers, *aunayan* the elder, was able to escape by bounding over the wall surrounding the field, but *ibuwan* was too short and could not escape. He was taken by the *raranges* to their *palakuwan* posting a guard outside house to prevent *ibuwan*'s escape.

aunayan was very worried about the safety of his little brother. He finally came up with a carefully considered plan. He would build a huge *tuwap* from strips of rattan wood and launch the kite from Fuyuan Mountain across the Beinan River.

One the day before *aunayan* planned to execute his plan, *aunayan* secretly went to the *raranges* village where he was able to evade the guards and let *ibuwan* know of the escape plan.

The next day, while still inside the *raranges' palakuwan*, *ibuwan* heard the buzzing "weng weng weng" sound of the kite and knew his brother was proceeding with the plan. The buzzing sound also attracted the attention of the *raranges* who were standing guard outside. The raranges rushed around to get a better look at this strange flying object. It was unlike anything they had ever seen and they all became very excited and couldn't stop chattering.

ibuwan said to the man guarding the *palakuwan* "What is that up in the air? Won't you let me get next to the window to take a closer look?" The guard agreed to let him come to the window.

When *ibuwan* was next to the window he said: "I still can't see very clearly from here. How about letting me go to the door where I can have a better view?" Once again the guard agreed to the request.

ibuwan stood in the doorway and watched the kite for a while and then said to the guard: "This is really too far away, couldn't you take me to the center of the plaza to watch the kite with the others?" Thinking there was no risk of *ibuwan* running away with so many *raranges* surrounding him in the plaza, the guard took *ibuwan*

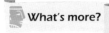 **What's more?**

> **tuwap:** this is a kite constructed of two rattan squares which are stacked to form an octagon, a shape of kite that scholars say is unique to Taiwan.
>
> **tabi:** Stone mortar. Many of these were discovered in the Beinan archeological excavations, however most of them were in the shape of a bowl.

out to watch the kite with the others. All were gathered around staring up into the sky.

Standing among the raranges, *ibuwan* said to the guard, "You know, I am really too short to see anything from here and all these people are blocking my view. Could you let me stand on that *tabi*?"

The guard then let *ibuwan* climb on to the *tabi* to better view the kite. The kite floated through the air bobbing up and down and all of the viewers were as if in a trance.

ibuwan then said: "What a strange thing that is, why don't you lend me your knife and I will cut the kite from the sky". The *raranges* guard didn't see any harm in letting him try, and everyone was curious to see how he would do it. He handed a knife to *ibuwan*.

Far away on Fuyuan Mountain aunayan could see all the *raranges* crowded together watching the kite. He pulled on the cord causing the kite to dip and climb. When the kite dipped a third time, *ibuwan* made as though he was going to slash the kite, but instead he thrust out his hand and grabbed on to the tail of the kite. In a moment, he was carried off into the sky, and when *aunayan* saw that *ibuwan* was on the kite he quickly pulled on the cord to guide his brother high in the sky above and away from the *raranges*.

Far and away *ibuwan* no longer needed the knife, so he let it drop to the ground. The falling knife pierced the belly of a pregnant woman below in the crowd. Her stomach split open and she gave birth to twins.

Finally, the *raranges* realized that this was all part of a plan for their prisoner to escape. It was too late to give chase – all they could was to watch him get away.

aunayan guided the kite to the top of Fuyuan Mountain on the north shore of the Beinan River. When *ibuwan* landed, *aunayan* discovered that the *raranges* had forced his brother to eat a whole manner of filthy and revolting things during his

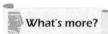

What's more?

Twins: for the Puyuma giving birth to twins is inauspicious.

kanaLeLya: this is also the Puyuma word for vomit. This small lake was located in Fuyuan village, Beinan township in Taidong, but because of road construction, the lake is no longer with us.

captivity. He felt pity for his brother but was also furious with the raranges. He had ibuwan purge all the things he had been forced to eat. The disgorged substances suddenly turned into a small lake. The Puyuma People call this lake kanaLeLya and although the lake is never dry; it gives off a strange odor.

Because of *ibuwan's* mistreatment by the *raranges*, the two brothers wanted to take revenge. They set off on a journey to babaTulan to seek advice from their maternal grandmother *taDanaw*.

After they told her of *ibuwan's* suffering at the hands of the *raranges*, *taDanaw* exclaimed: "Let the eternal night fall upon the *raranges*" whereupon the world became swallowed up in darkness.

However, even in the darkness the *raranges* were able to find wood for building fires with which to cook their food and warm their bodies. The darkness didn't really affect them. On the contrary, it was very inconvenient for the brothers and their own people.

The brothers went back to *taDanaw* and told her: "The raranges are getting along fine while it is we who suffer. How can we bring back the daylight?"

taDanaw said: "In that case, go to Dulan Mountain and borrow a white *turukuk* from the elders who live there. Let the *turukuk* call out three times and there will be daylight."

The brothers followed *taDanaw's* instructions and the light returned. The brothers however were still not satisfied, as they had not gained their revenge on the *raranges*. They returned to *taDanaw* to seek her advice on how to destroy the *raranges*.

"Very well", said *taDanaw*, "Go to the outer realms and create an earthquake!"

The brothers then busily moved stones all around *taDanaw's* home so that it would be protected from the coming earthquake. They propped flat stones all around the house and wrapped the betel nut trees in steel plates then bound the trees together with rope.

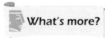 **What's more?**

babaTulan: this is located in the present day location of the Beinan excavation site in Taidong County.

turukuk: chicken.

After the brothers had done everything possible to secure taDanaw's home, they said to her: "When you hear the sound of thunder you will know we have arrived in the outer realms."

aunayan and *ibuwan* went to the heavens to prepare for the thunderstorms and earthquakes. The iron plates rattled, as fire, earthquakes and other calamities engulfed the earth. The conflagration destroyed all but *taDanaw's* house.

After this went on for some time, *taDanaw* exclaimed to the brothers: "Enough, enough!. The *raranges* have been wiped out the thunderstorms and earthquakes may cease."

The brothers did as they were told and the earthquakes and other catastrophes came to a halt. The *raranges* homeland, *talalabuwan* was reduced to ashes with only some stone slabs left standing.

These remains, the Crescent Pillars of the Beinan Ruins, are all that is left of this incident. The raranges were completed wiped out.

This story tells us why the *Puyuma* treat their ancestral grounds, the homeland of the raranges, *talalabuwan*, as a restricted sacred ground.

Where did it come from?

This story was told by Lin Jen-cheng of the Baosang village in Taidong City, collected and edited by the anthropologist Sung Lung-sheng, with advice from the elder Chen Kuang-jung.

What's more?

talalabuwan: Ruins. It refers to the site of the Beinan ruins, and the Puyuma people have always considered it to be a sacred but forbidden place. They believe that places where people have died are inhabited by evil spirits and warn their offspring to stay away; it is also a reminder to succeeding generations to avoid allowing such disasters to recur.

Crescent Stone Pillars: in the Beinan excavation site there are many large stone pillars which were likely part of some sort of building. What their use was exactly is still debated but recent theories are that these were central columns of structures.

Origins of the Rites of Giving Thanks to the Sea

The Nanwang Villagers have celebrations in different locations every year after the millet harvest. They carry millet to the ocean and to the north shores of the Beinan River to present their offerings. This celebration and the gratitude the people feel for the harvest has been transmitted from generation to generation.

A special celebration of the Nanwang Village, called "Rites of the Sea"(*mulali-yaban*), is unique. No other group within the Puyuma has this festival. It is performed after the summer millet harvest. The people go to perform rites of gratitude to their ancestors at different locations: on the ocean shores facing Orchid Island (*buTul*) and Green Island (*sanasan*), and along the north shore of the Beinan River facing Dulan Mountain.

Why are these rites performed at the same time at three places? Because the Rites of the Sea originate from three different legends and traditions that were passed down from the ancestors of the Nanwang villagers.

Rites of the Sea (1)

In Search of the Millet Seed

Many years before there were any historical records, an ancestor of the Nanwang village named *demaLasaw* went out to the eastern seas in search of a plant that could be a staple part of his people's food.

One day he came to buTul where he fell in love with a beautiful woman named *tayban*. *tayban* also fell in love with the young and handsome *demaLasaw*. She agreed to marry him.

But even after the two were married, *demaLasaw* did not forget his original purpose in travelling the seas. He searched all over *buTul* and discovered a group of people who ate a precious grain they called *dawa* (millet). *demaLasaw* and *tayban* planned to take the *dawa* to *demaLasaw's* village on Taiwan.

However, the people of *buTul* highly prized *dawa* and strictly forbid its being taken off the island.

demaLasaw and *tayban* tried to think of ways they could hide the seed. They tried their armpits, their hair, their eyelids, ears, mouth and nose, but each time they tried to leave the island with the hidden dawa they were discovered. And each time the *dawa* was confiscated.

Although they failed so many attempts, they never gave up. Finally, *demaLasaw* came up with a plan. He would hide the *dawa* in his private parts. The plan worked and they were able to take the *dawa* back to their village. This is how *dawa* came to the Puyuma.

demaLasaw and tayban left *buTul* with *tayban's* elder brother, *umaluDaw*. However *umaluDaw* was not away from home for long before he missed *buTul* so much that he decided to return.

On the evening before his return to *buTul*, *umaluDaw* asked *demaLasaw* and *tayban* to promise that every year they would perform a ceremony in honor of *buTul* as the origin of *dawa*. Every year after the millet harvest they executed the ceremony by making offerings of millet wine and millet porridge at the ocean shore facing *buTul*.

demaLasaw and *tayban* strictly observed this custom. Every year following the harvest they took millet products to the edge of the ocean to perform the ceremony showing gratitude for the harvest and asking for abundance in the years to come.

demaLasaw and *tayban* are the ancestors of the *sapayan* and *ra'ra'* clans of the Nanwang Village. To this day, these two clans perform the *buTul* millet ceremonies.

Where did it come from?
This story was told by Chen Kuang-jung, chairperson of the Nanwang Community Development Association in Taidong City.

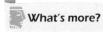 **What's more?**

Millet harvest: every year in the middle of July millet matures and is ideal for harvesting.

Rites of the Sea (2)

Giving Thanks to the Great Fish

Among the *arasis* clan of the Nanwang village *patakiu* was famous for being a great trickster.

One of *patakiu's* favorite tricks was to steal rice dough patties. When the people of his village were preparing the patties, patakiu would loudly shout "fire" and ask for the people to come and help. When everyone rushed off to find the fire, *patakiu* went into the kitchen and took all of the patties.

After this happened several times, *patakiu's* neighbors discovered the trick. They were very upset and stormed off to *patakiu's* family to complain.

patakiu's behavior was very distressing and shameful for his family. However, even though they repeatedly scolded him, *patakiu* continued to play tricks whenever he could. *kuLaLui*, *patakiu's* maternal uncle, told the neighbors of his plan to banish *patakiu* to a faraway place. *patakiu* would not be able to return to their village, and would no longer cause trouble.

One-day *kuLaLui* and the other males of the village took *patakiu* hunting on *sanasan*.

In those days there was a huge banyan tree that spanned the gap between Taiwan and *sanasan*. To get to *sanasan* the people would simply cross the banyan tree root bridge.

When they arrived on *sanasan, kuLaLiu* directed the hunters to go into the wilds to scare the animals out into the open where they could surround and capture them. *patakiu* enthusiastically joined in the hunt by going deep into the bush to chase out the animals. He never suspected that this was a trap set by his family and friends!

What's more?

Piling rice: the word for pestle in the Puyuma language is "rasuk" and for mortar" tabi" and the word for pounding milled or rice is "ma Tinapan".

sanasan: this refers to Green Island, located in the Pacific Ocean off the coast of Taidong county.

When *patakiu* was on the island deep in the jungle, the others all ran back across the bridge to the main island of Taiwan. They then chopped away the *banyan* tree root bridge, leaving *patakiu* stranded on the island. At last, that troublesome trickster would no longer bother their village!

It was some time before *patakiu* discovered that he had been left behind. Without any idea of the plan to desert him, he went about his hunting. But when he made his way back to the banyan tree bridge and found it was gone he knew that something was wrong. He had been exiled by his fellow tribesmen! *patakiu* looked out over the vast sea and let out a cry of despair and sadness.

patakiu's wailing stirred the sympathies of the gods.

The gods knew that *patakiu* had been left to wander endlessly on his own. They knew he wasn't really a bad person, so they ordered a great fish to carry him back to his home. Before starting the journey, the great fish said to *patakiu* "Hold your breath when we go under the water. When you can hold it no more pinch my gill and I will come to the surface so you can breathe; when we arrive at the shore and you want to get off, pinch me three times."

After three deep dives they arrived at the coast near Maoshan on the eastern shores of Taiwan. *patakiu* pinched the great fish three times and the fish flopped its tail to send *patakiu* flying onto the sandy shores. This is how *patakiu* returned home safe and sound.

Once on the shore *patakiu* was unable to stand steady. When he got up, he would wobble and then fall over. His people gave him a new nickname *aliTaliT* which means "the-one-who-falls-over".

After the giant fish left *patakiu* on the shore, and was swimming out to the ocean, it turned around and said: "Every year at millet harvest time, you shall come to shores to make an offering to me to commemorate this event".

From this time on, *patakiu* no longer caused trouble or played tricks. Every year all of the adult male members of the *arasis* clan that are descended from *patakiu* make the journey past Maoshan to the ocean shores across from *sanasan*. There they give thanks to the great fish for having saved the life of *patakiu*.

Where did it come from?

This story was told by Chen Kuang-jung, chairperson of the Nanwang Community Development Association in Taidong City.

Rites of the Sea (3)

New Rice to Feed Myaibar the Mountain Spirit

An ancestor of the *pasara'aT* clan used to wade across the Beinan River to the northern shore. There he tended to their crops and cut and gathered wood for his people's fires and buildings. One day while he was eating lunch he discovered a *maiDang* in the food bag hanging from the ox cart.

He was so startled that he tipped over the rice bag. As he thought about this bad omen it suddenly occurred to him that because the Rites to the Sea would take place in a few days, it might be disrespectful to the spirits to wade across the Beinan River. He decided to offer some of the summer harvest to appease *myaibar*, otherwise, he thought, even though the river is quite shallow, an accident might happen.

From this day on, every year on the day of the sea festival, the descendants of the *pasara'aT* clan and their relatives, the *balangatu* clan, cross the Beinan River to the north shore where they make offerings to thank *myaibar*.

Where did it come from?

This story was told by Chen Kuang-jung, chairperson of the Nanwang Community Development Association in Taidong City.

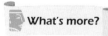 What's more?

maiDang: *Deinagkistrodon acutus* also known *inter alia* as the hundred pace snake or Chinese moccasin.

myaibar: the spirit who controls the mountains.

達悟族
T　a　o

01

The Bamboo Man and the Stone Man: The Creation Story of the Tao

> A group of odd-looking people with even stranger movements spread throughout the land. Before long, a great flood came and covered the entire island and all of these strange people. Nine years later, spring finally returned and the people of the heaven sent two children, the man of bamboo and the man of stone.
>
> These two were to carry on the lifeline of the Tao and to introduce them to the necessary wisdom, knowledge, and skills for living, and also to caution the people of all generations to respect the heavens and cherish all things of this earth.

In the great and vast Pacific Ocean there is a mysterious and wonderful place known as Orchid Island. In the waters surrounding the island are all kinds of fish and beautiful shellfish. The trees on the island grow tall and the vegetation is lush. Everywhere one can see beautiful orchids, lilies, wild chrysanthemums and other rich and varied plants. There are also the *pahabahad*, the cute and cuddly *votdak* and the *totowo*, which only comes out at night.

One day a very strange event occurred. An unusually shaped boat suddenly appeared in the ocean coming toward Orchid Island. The two ends of the boat were pointed and the boat's body was in the shape of a "U". The boat slowly made its way to the mysterious island.

When the boat reached the island shores a group of strange-looking people disembarked on to the island. They didn't look like people, didn't look like spirits, and didn't look like ghosts! Some had very broad and powerful-looking shoulders, while some had eyes that seemed to pop out of their faces. Some had huge hands but tiny feet. This strange collection of people found this beautiful island to be a very attractive place to live, so they decided to settle here.

Their way of living was very different from normal people and each of them had some strange and special faculties.

One of them was called *Si-paloy*. Every time *Si-paloy* had a different opinion than someone else there would be a confrontation and *Si-paloy* would get beaten up

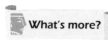

What's more?

pongso: Orchid Island is located off the coast of Taitung in eastern Taiwan. At sunset the rock formations near the island's northwest side resemble the caricature of an American indian, thus the old name for the island was "Red Head Island". In 1946 the government named the island "Orchid Island" after the area was discovered to be rich in Moth orchids (*Phalaenopsis*). Orchid Island is Taiwan's second largest offshore island.

tamek or kochozang in Japanese: many species of Orchid's are threatened with extinction, and are now protected.

pahabahad: the birdwing butterfly (*Troides magellanus*) is Taiwan's largest butterfly and in Taiwan is found only on Orchid Island. It is seriously endangered due to overdevelopment.

votdak or panganpen: the fruit wolf (*Paguma larvata*) is known by either of these names in the Tao language. It is endangered, and while it looks quite cute, the Tao consider this animal to be raised by evil spirits.

totowo: Scops owl (*Otus elegans botelensis*) comes directly from the animal's call. It is a nocturnal bird and perhaps only 1000 remained in 2002. The Tao believe totowo to be an incarnation of evil spirits because their favored habitat is on the branches of what the Tao consider to be an inauspicious tree, the sea poison tree (*Barringtonia asiatica*).

tatala: the name for the very specific type of canoe made by the Tao. Boat they make, boats made by others than the Tao are called *avang*.

very badly. But *Si-paloy* was able to come back from the dead and was able to live in the sea as well as on the land.

Another one, *Si-ozamen*, neither raised crops nor fished in the sea. It seemed as though he needed nothing to eat.

One day the tall and powerful *Si-kaleted* summoned all the people on the island together to announce, "My name is *Si-kaleted* and I want to make the sky higher because now it is too low". He then made the sky so high that no person could touch it.

Then there was *Si-pacilalaw*. Whenever *Si-pacilalaw* saw a fat little baby or a woman carrying a child he would act as though preparing to eat them.

These are but a few examples of the strange circumstances of Orchid's Island.

After these strange people arrived on the beautiful island, the trees and plants no longer flourished as before, and the birds no longer sang their happy songs. Before long, a great flood came inundating the entire island and all these strange people.

Nine years passed before the people in the heavens allowed this little island to emerge from the floodwaters and recover its lush trees and other foliage. The people of the heavens enhanced the island's beauty by bestowing it with precious orchids, owls, and butterflies.

Seeing the recovery of the island's magnificence, the people of the heavens sent two sons on a mission: one son to descend upon a large stone in the *Iratay* village who would be known as "the man born of stone" and the other to descend into the bamboo of the *Imowrod* village who would be known as "the man born of bamboo".

The people of the heavens had endowed both bamboo man and stone man with special magical powers. A male or female child could be born from any part of their

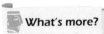

What's more?

anito: we Tao have two types of "ghosts": 1) spirts of deceased people, and 2) devils or evil spirits.

Si-paloy: for the names of unmarried persons the Tao insert "*Si*" in front of their name, as here with *Si-paloy*, or another example is *Si-naban*.

bodies. However, once they had given birth to a boy and a girl, their magical powers would dissipate and they would be the same as any other ordinary person.

Time passed and what was said of the children bestowed with magical powers by
people in the heavens all proved to be true. The bamboo man of *Imowrod* village
effortlessly gave birth to a son and a daughter who grew to adulthood, married
and had children. The strange thing was that all of their children were blind or de-
formed, they were retarded, would die prematurely, or just would not grow.

The same situation was true of the stone man. As with the bamboo man, all his
children were abnormal.

One day the bamboo man and the stone man met by chance at the ocean where
they had gone to fish. As they were talking about matters concerning their children
and grandchildren, they devised a plan to have their children marry one another to
see if it might improve the situation.

Many years passed and their hunch turned out to be correct: the children were now
all intelligent, talented and healthy, bringing solace to all.

The bamboo man and the stone man presented wisdom, knowledge and skills to
future generations. They taught the women how to cultivate yam and taro, how to
recognize plants, and how to weave cloth; they taught the men how to fish and how
to help the women care for the fields. Even more importantly, they taught them
how to protect their beautiful island.

The bamboo man and the stone man gave the people their most solemn advice, "No
matter what you do, do not waste anything. Use only those resources that you need

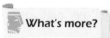

What's more?

Iratay: refers to what today is known as the *Iratay* village in Lanyu Township, Taitung County.

Imowrod: refers to what today is known as the *Imowrod* village in Lanyu
Township, Taitung County.

amyan do vahey: the story tells of how any part of the bodies of the bamboo and stone people can give birth to children. Another version has it that
only after rubbing the knees can there be a birth. *Tao* believe that following
the birth of a child, it should be named and blessed at dawn because the
sunrise symbolizes a good beginning.

and do not spoil anything the creator has bestowed."

To protect the island they laid down customs and rules that would be the foundation for managing the island. They named the island *pongso no tao*.

Where did it come from?

This story was told by Si-yapen Maraos a female elder from Iratay Village, Lanyu Township, Taidong County who at the time (circa 2002) was seventy-eight years old.

What's more?

misin mo: In the early morning of the day selected as auspicious by the bride and groom's parents for the wedding ceremony, the man, dressed in ceremonial robes and a gold necklace, bracelet, helmut and carrying a sword, will go to the brides home and together they will enjoy tarot and pork.

sosoli: wetland taro is one of the most commonly cultivated plants on Orchid Island.

tominon: weaving represents a woman's social status, Tao women do most of their weaving during the autumn and winter.

ni mangamawog a tao: the creator is a Tao prophet and does not refer to Jesus.

pongso (bongso) no tao: literally means the island where people live.

mizezyaka libangbang

> As the moon shines over the ocean, the flying fish are attracted to the fires of the Tao, and one by one they jump into the boats. The flying fish season of pongso no tao has arrived! Long ago the Tao did not understand the ways of the flying fish, and when they ate the flying fish they would break out in a rash.
>
> Through a dream, mizezyaka libangbang, the flying fish spirit, taught one of the Tao how to catch and eat the flying fish. From that time on, the Tao not only learned the joys of the flying fish, they also learned to treasure everything of the sea.

The ancestors of the *Tao* made their livelihood from fishing in the ocean, collecting shellfish and planting mountain yam and taro. They solemnly thanked the creator for the gifts and blessings of the earth and for letting them enjoy a life free from hunger and hardship.

The Tao live on Orchid Island surrounded by the Pacific Ocean. They have a deep understanding and love of the sea. Of all the many species of fish of the ocean they have particularly special feelings for the *alibangbang*, or what is known as the flying fish.

Spreading their wings to hover over the ocean waters, the flying fish are said to have been a gift to the *Tao* from *mizezyaka libangbang*, the flying fish spirit. But

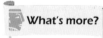

What's more?

inapo: Tao do not have the custom of maintaining graves. Rather every year around the eleventh month when worshiping gods, they pay homage to their departed relatives.

when the *Tao* ate the flying fish with other foods they developed uncomfortable and untreatable sores. So, for a time they decided to stop eating the flying fish.

mizezyaka libangbang was very upset to find that the *Tao* didn't know how to eat or prepare the flying fish. The spirit came up with an ingenious plan on how to demonstrate to the Tao the intrinsic absolute value of everything made by the creator. The plan would reveal to the Tao the proper way to eat flying fish.

mizezyaka libangbang spoke to a *Tao* elder through the elder's dreams, "I am the flying fish spirit and I want you to instruct your people that from now they must obey every word I say and every rule I make down to the finest detail. You must treasure and love the flying fish, you must not waste anything that the creator has bestowed upon you, respect the flying fish, do not make me sad or unhappy."

The elder said, "We are sorry, but we did not mean any disrespect to the flying fish. It is just that when we eat it all over our bodies we break out in an uncomfortable and untreatable rash."

mizezyaka libangbang responded:" Now I am going to tell you how to eat the flying fish so that you will no longer develop a rash. You must remember every word I say. Do not overlook anything because this will be very important for the rules and lives of your tribe for generations to come."

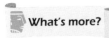

What's more?

alibangbang: Tao classify flying fish into the following four categories:

1. White-winged flying fish are the first flying fish of the season to enter the waters near Orchid Island, they are attracted to bright light and are the main species caught during the flying fish season.

2. Red-winged flying fish are most numerous and are identified by yellowish-brown spots on their fins. Pregnant women should not eat these lest they bear children prone to rash.

3. Black-winged flying fish are relatively scarce, and are regarded by Tao as the most precious and great flying fish. Roasting of these fish for eating is not advised as otherwise one will develop sores.

4. Purple-spotted fin flying fish is the most abundant and also the most favored of Tao; it is relatively small in size and can be eaten by children.

The elder said, "Please go ahead. I will listen carefully and will tell all of our people that your words must be strictly followed."

mizezyaka libangbang then began," Every year when the flying fish are about to arrive you must perform a ceremony in their honor. The women shall go to the mountains to dig up the mountain yam and taro, and the men shall chop wood and prepare racks for the flying fish. On the first day of *mirayon*, men and women shall divide their duties. All shall celebrate in earnest the abundance of flying fish for the year, and call for overcoming all ocean currents and other adversities, you shall all pray for your peoples' peace and good health."

mizezyaka libangbang patiently explained each point in detail to the *Tao*, "When her husband goes to the sea to fish, the wife must catch sand crabs, for this will relieve some of his hardship. The husband will bring back and cook the flying fish for his wife and children. When there are too many flying fish, the whole family shall help with cleaning the flying fish, and then they should be dried and stored. The husband shall instruct the wife and children that the flying fish shall not be eaten outdoors, and when one is full from eating one will say to everyone, 'I have eaten my fill, but everyone please continue to eat.' When finished eating one must always wash one's hands."

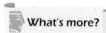

What's more?

mizezyaka libangbang: the flying fish spirit in Tao lore is said to have taught the Tao all kinds of protocol related to how to catch the fish.

Developing sores: the stories of the Tao tell us that flying fish cannot be consumed with other foods and cannot be roasted.

kamanrarakeh: the Tao do not have a system of chiefs, classes or social inequality. When a major event or conflict occurs the elders of each village congregate to discuss. Although the villages do not have a clear leader, those who possess extraordinary skills such as with a knife, an axe, or deftness with certain crafts, are often deemed as temporary leaders.

mirayon: the name of the flying fish ceremony; the season for fishing is from March to June of the solar calender.

zazawan: rack for drying flying fish.

mitawaz so libangbang: one method of fishing for flying fish is using torches at night to attract the fish into the fishers' nets.

"During the flying fish season you must not say anything unlucky or scold others. Also, because this is the season for the flying fish only, you must not catch any other kind of fish. You must not be too greedy when you catch the flying fish, just take enough to last you for the year."

"After the season has passed, everyone shall get together to celebrate, sing and dance in honor of the great harvest and in honor of peace. On this day of celebration, the yam, taro, and dried fish should all be shared with relatives and friends. In particular, you must share these things with people who have no family and with families who are unable to go into the sea to fish. In this way your tribe will have fish to eat every year, and by helping one another, your children and grandchildren will enjoy prosperity forever."

After *mizezyaka libangbang* had finished, the elder awoke. He went from his bedroom out to the *panadngan* where he sat facing the sea thinking about all he had been told in the dream. He believed that everything the Flying Fish Spirit had said was true. How could we bear to waste anything that the sea has given to us?

What's more?

teyngi: during the flying fish season women cannot casually leave their homes because they must prepare the appurtenances and foods for the flying fish rites, and they must dig up land crabs for their husbands who are hard at work fishing.

Eating etiquette among the Tao: from the eldest of the elders, down through the younger generation, one by one, the meal is eaten and when satiated, the elder politely announces "I have eaten my fill, thank you."

waganam: there are different dances for men and women. For men the "warrior dance" is where they wear a thong and have nothing covering their strong bare chests. The primal roar drives precise and powerful dance steps as they alternate between squatting, jumping and twirling. When performing the "hair dance", women wear a dress of white background, and blue and black stripes. Singing and dancing they lower and lift their heads so their long hair flows like the ocean waves.

Unable to go to sea: refers to those in mourning or people with debilities that prevent them from going out to sea.

The next day the elder told the people of his village all he had learned from *mizezyaka libangbang*. When he had finished, all the people nodded their heads and agreed to abide by the teachings. This is the origin of the festival to honor the Flying Fish Spirit *mizezyaka libangbang*. Every year when the Tao perform this ceremony it is as though they are paying honoring all life, a demonstration of their love for nature and their respect for, and awe of, the creator.

Where did it come from?

This story was told by Ms. Si-yapen Pazpazen of Iran-meylek Village, Lanyu Township, Taidong County.

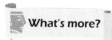

What's more?

rahet, angsa, oyod: In the eating culture of the Tao men, elders, and women all eat a different kind of fish, a kind of wisdom that derives from a scarcity of resources in the past. The fish eaten by males is called *rahet.* in principal elders may eat any kind of fish and the fish they do eat is called *angsa*, an example being mahi mahi or common dolphinfish. Fish eaten by females is *oyod*, somewhat more delicate, such as the grouper, in particular for pregnant or nursing women when more nutrition is needed. So the fish eaten by women is somewhat selective. However, as times change and resources are no longer scarce, these distinctions disappear.

panadngan: "backrest stone" refers to two long, upright flat stones placed in the front of the traditional Tao dwelling. The stones are like the backrests of chairs and people often sit in the yard cooling off and having a chat with their backs against the stones.

03

Origins of the Tao Canoe

> The *Tao* followed the water cave to the land of the underworld. What they found there was both surprising and pleasing. Men and women were working together in their own special areas of expertise and everything was very orderly. But it was the very finely built canoes that really opened their eyes.
>
> The people of the underworld transferred their skills of building the boats, but more important they also helped the *Tao* understand the keys to successfully making the boats: careful use of resources, cooperation and mutual aid, and a spirit of contributing to the common good.

There once was an exceedingly smart and charming rat who had been transformed from a man of the underworld and sent by the heavens to live among the *Tao*.

The people of the underworld and the *Tao* were all beings of the ocean. Their customs and ways of living were very similar and communication between the groups was very smooth.

Although the *Tao* were quite adept at making boats, their skills were nowhere near the boat-making craft of the people of the underworld. When the *Tao* went fishing their catch was small and their boats often leaked. And so it was that the people of the heavens decided to dispatch the rat from the underworld to live among the *Tao* and teach them the art of making boats.

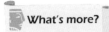 **What's more?**

mitatala: the Tao techniques of constructing canoes are detailed below.

The rat of the underworld got along very well with the Tao. They exchanged all kinds of life experiences and ideas. After some time had passed the people of the underworld led a group of twelve *Tao* through the water caves, *tozngan no ranom*, to their home in the underworld.

"Wow, there are so many people here. More than our tribe!"

This was the first time that *Tao* people visited the underworld. They were very excited and curious, looking all about at the new sights. The people here were very happy and harmonious. The women planted yam and taro and wove cloth. Men specialized in wood-working and the art of boat-building. The boats they built were both beautiful and very technically advanced.

But their language sounded like "Weng, Weng, Weng!" How peculiar!

One of the older people of the underworld warmly greeted the *Tao* visitors. He showed them around introducing the Tao to their culture and daily lives.

"Sharing is an essential part of our daily life," he said, "while we loathe selfish people, we really like completing something together."

"Our ancestors taught us that we must not over-harvest the trees because if the forests are gone, not only will there be floods and landslides, we will also have no wood for our boats. It will then be impossible to enjoy the rich bounty of the sea."

"When fishing, we must only catch enough to feed our family. We also select the proper lands to plant yam and taro as these are our staple foods and are essential for our rituals and ceremonies. These are the main differences between our people of the underworld and your people!"

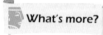 **What's more?**

tozngan no ranom: the water caves of this story have never been found on Orchid Island.

transfer of boat building technology: another version of this story has a person from the underworld transformed into a rat who then lures a Tao child into the underworld to gain new knowledge, and during the course of this learning the child intuits the boat building technology.

Item by item the elder gaved detailed description of life in the underworld. The *Tao* listened attentively to the words of the elder. They greatly respected the underworld people's way of taking care and using their natural environment, and realized only by protecting the forests, soil and sea would they be able to leave behind a beautiful world for their children and grandchildren.

One *Tao* was especially anxious to know more about their boats. He asked, "How do you build such exquisite and sturdy boats?"

The elder of the underworld smiled, saying "You can see for yourself. Let me show you where our people make these boats. "

The *Tao* asked another question, "No matter how we make our boats, they are easily damaged. They are unsteady and it is difficult to navigate the ocean."

The elder said, "It indeed is not easy to make a boat that is both beautiful and sturdy. We too once experienced what you describe. But later the people of the heavens told our ancestors, 'Building boats is a part of nature, you must honor the creator and the natural environment where you live, and then your actions will conform with the creator's intent.' After we were told this, the people in the heavens taught our ancestors all the skills they needed to build boats. We have been building our boats for generations based on these instructions."

The people of the underground didn't forget to remind the *Tao*, "Building a boat is a very serious and sacred matter. It can only be accomplished through the cooperation of men and women performing specified work."

The people of the underworld then said to the *Tao* women. "*Tao* women shall diligently cultivate the fields and plant yam, taro, mountain-yam, and millet. Moreover, you should frequently remove weeds from the fields so that the crops will be healthy and fruitful. The women should also pay special attention to raising pigs and goats because there are sacrifices that are attendant to the ceremony of the boats, and after the ceremony you shall make gifts of these offerings to your friends and relatives."

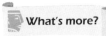 **What's more?**

karatayan: each of the *Tao* villages has its own fishing grounds, pastures and gardens which people from other villages may not enter or use.

The people of the underworld then said to the men, "The men shall help the women plow the fields. All they plant will be used in the boat ceremony rituals. This is most important."

The people of the underworld took the *Tao* to see how they built their boats. There were many groups of builders working together to make the beautiful boats. One of the leaders explained the methods and art of boat-building "There are a number of taboos and rules to follow when making a boat. "

"First, in order to respect the forests, before starting to make the boat, the tribe must discuss what tree to use. One of the experienced elders shall select the wood for the boat."

"Second, you cannot say anything unlucky or scold people. If you utter bad words, fishing from this boat will be poor."

"Third, if a builder experiences misfortune or a member of the family dies, then the work should stop and they should grieve for the dead."

The elder continued to talk in detail about the boat building. "When the boat is finished there shall be a ceremony for the boat's first contact with water. At the ceremony yam and taro are loaded into the boat and the blood of the domestic animals is to be used to anoint the boat while everyone sings and dances in praise of the vessel. This will bring good luck and fortune. At this time you should invite your friends and relatives to come and enjoy the ceremony."

After learning everything about the boats the *Tao* went back to their village carrying their gifts of yam, taro, pigs and goats. They shared these gifts as they told

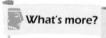 **What's more?**

Burial customs of the Tao: often the family of the departed will surround the house with wooden slats and place wooden slats along the sides of the route to the burial site. The burials generally take in a place next to the sea to the left of the village.

yami keyteytetngehan: in the past *Tao* would regularly build large boats every three or six years. If diligently maintained the boats could be used for as long as six years.

their fellow villagers everything about their visit to the underworld. From this time on the *Tao* used their experience and the lessons from the underworld to build their own lives and culture. They also built the beautifully shaped and sturdy boats *tatala no tao*.

But for some reason, and no one seems to know why, after this contact between the *Tao* and the people of the underworld, there are no more stories or news of mutual contacts or relations.

Where did it come from?

This story was told by Mr. Si-yapen Pazpazen of Iran-meylek Village, Lanyu Township, Taidong County.

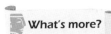 **What's more?**

yamapalwas: when construction of a large *tatala* is complete and before its first contact with water *Tao* perform a ceremony in reverence to the spirit of the boat and to exorcise any evil spirits that might interfere with its smooth operation and bountiful catch of fish.

rala: many rites and ceremonies use the blood of chickens or pigs.

masipangarilow: sharing is deeply ingrained in *Tao* culture and things such as dried fish, yam and taro are often given away to others.

tatala no tao: for the *Tao*, a maritime people the boat is their primary transportation as well as used for fishing. In the past all males must learn the craft of boat building if they wanted to have any standing in society. The *Tao* vessel is made be splicing together pieces of wood and thus differs from e.g., dugout canoes which are made from one piece of carved out wood. While the structures of the small (1, 2, or 3 seats) and large (6, 8, or 10 seats) *tatala no tao* are the same, the small ones are comprised of 21 pieces of wood while the large are comprised of 27 pieces.

The Child of ango

> The sounds of an infant crying emerged from the *ango* forest. Fortunately, the heavens had taken pity on this child and he was discovered by an old man and woman who would raise him as their own. When he grew older he was hard-working and filial.
>
> It wasn't until his birth mother recognized him that he finally learned the truth.
>
> He selected the best pig and goat and put on a great feast. Among the Tao, this is the greatest way to demonstrate honor. The feast was to honor the old man and woman, but he also invited his birth mother to join. Not only did he treat the old man and woman who raised him with all due honor and respect, he harbored no any resentment toward his birth mother who had abandoned him.

There once was a young man in a *Tao* village who was very intelligent, nice-looking, good-natured and very respectful to his parents and family. However, he had a most unusual background.

Many years before, a young unmarried woman had became pregnant. The villagers all suspected the woman of having done something she shouldn't have. She was shunned by all.

With the whole village suspecting her and vicious rumors about her running rampant, the young woman was loath to go out from her home during the day. She only went out at night. But as her belly swelled with child, she became even more afraid of going out and stayed hidden away all the time.

When she felt the child coming she went to a deserted place and gave birth to a healthy and chubby baby boy. His eyes were bright and very cute. However, because he had no father, the woman was afraid that the people in the village would not welcome this cute little child. Not knowing what to do and desperate, she asked her mother to abandon the child in the dark of the night.

The young woman's mother left the child in an *ango* grove far from her village.

In another part of the village there lived a kind old man and his wife. They had been married for many years but had no children. They always wanted a child, but the heavens had decided this was not to be.

On the same evening as the child had been abandoned, the old man went out to the sea to cast his fishing nets. Just as he was approaching the grove of *ango*, he suddenly heard cries "Wahhh, Wahhh!" coming from the forest. Curious as to what this might be, he ran over to where the noise was coming from. There he found the little baby boy. He was surprised and overjoyed. He said, "Aii, such a cute little baby. Who could be so cruel as to leave you here alone among the *ango* trees?"

The old man tenderly picked up the infant and carried him home. When he arrived he cheerfully announced to his wife, "I didn't catch any fish today, but see what I did find - a cute little baby boy alone among the *ango*!"

As soon as she saw the little child she fell in love, "This is heaven's gift to us!"

The old man reminded his wife, "You must drink lots of water so you will have plenty of milk."

All the time the child was growing up the old couple carefully attended to all his needs. Seeing the child dashing about the old couples' garden, the neighbors thought this was odd, "Strange! That couple has been married for so many years

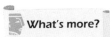

What's more?

kekey: Prior to being given a name children are all called "kekey." Tao follow the system known as teknonymy whereby the parent is named after the child. After a married couple has their first child, the parents give up their original names and the father's name becomes "Siaman-OOO", while the mother's name becomes "Sinan-OOO" with the child's name following.

ango: this large perennial evergreen tree grows in large clusters and is a member of the family Pandanacea, genus *Pandanus* and is often known in English as the "Screw Pine". The edges and undersides of the leaves have hard sharp thorns. There are still many ango groves on Orchid Island. The Tao people often use the plant's aerial roots to make racks to dry fish.

but never had children. They are so old now? Who is that youngster running around their home?"

As the child grew older he went to the sea to help with fishing and to the mountains to help the old couple with cultivating the yam and taro fields.

But when he played with the children in the village they would laugh and make fun of him, saying, "You were not borne by your parents, you were found abandoned in the *ango* grove."

He angrily retorted: "I am my mother's child and I was weaned on my mother's milk. My parents love me very much."

Every time he played with the other boys they would taunt him with the same words and each time he would get into a fight. And each time he came home confused, his mother would just kiss him tenderly and reassure him, "Of course you are my dear child."

As years went by the boy matured in understanding and took on the responsibility of his home with great diligence and attention. Although the villagers would still deride him, "You are not your parents' child", he no longer was bothered or became angry.

The child grew up to be a handsome and bright young man. When he was older he continued to go to the sea to fish, to the mountains to pick taro, yam, and to feed the domestic animals.

One day he was going to the mountains to till the fields. He came across a middle aged woman who seemed very familiar. As he got closer to the woman, she exclaimed, "My child! You are my child! I am your mother!"

"I am not your child, my mother is at home!" While his voice was loud and confident, in his heart he was very troubled. The woman just would not give up. Every

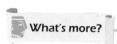

What's more?

maka veyvow: upon reaching adulthood, the *Tao* have no rite of passage as such. Rather, the determination of maturity is based on one's skills. For men, this would be his skill as a fisher and his participation in all sorts of community matters large and small, while for the women, the determination would be based upon how she handles affairs of the household, her planting yam and taro, trapping crabs, and so on.

time she saw the young man she would pester him.

Finally, when he couldn't stand the woman bothering him any longer, he asked his mother, "Mama, are you my birth mother? Why does some woman claiming to be my mother keep bothering me?"

His mother wiped tears from her eyes as she looked at the young man who she had nurtured from the abandoned baby found by her husband. They had raised him as their own child. She said, "Son, you are grown up now. I can't hide this matter from you any longer. It is for you to make your own decisions and judgments." The old man and woman then told him the story from beginning to end.

In *Tao* society to slaughter a *pig* or a *goat* and hold a feast for friends and relatives is one of the most honorable things a person can do for another. It is also the best way to show respect and honor for one's parents.

To show his appreciation for the kindness of the old couple, who had raised him, the young man selected the biggest and fattest pig and goat to slaughter at the time of *apiya vehan*. He then invited all his friends and relatives to share in the celebration in honor of the old couple.

The young man also invited his birth mother to the celebration. But he gave her only the smallest portion, saving the largest and fattest part of the meat for the old couple that had raised him.

Where did it come from?

This story was told by Si-yapen Maraos a female Elder from Iratay Village, Lanyu Township, Taitung County who at the time of telling the story (circa 2002), was seventy eight years old.

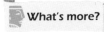 ### What's more?

Pigs, Goats: *Tao* raise their pigs as family members, letting them freely roam and graze around their households. There are very few actual pens for the pigs and the goats are entirely free to roam about. Goats are identified by an ear tag so there is no concern about theft. *Tao* do not use pigs and goats on a daily basis, rather they are slaughtered just for celebrations and special occasions.

apiya vehan: *Tao* consider auspicious times to be during the full moon or early morning.

|製作群亮相|

✦ 阿美族

故事採集者：

馬耀・基朗 Mayaw Kilang

漢名：陳俊男。政治大學民族學博士。出生於花蓮市，屬於撒奇萊雅人（Sakizaya）。小時候因為父親工作的關係，走遍了台灣西部地區，後來為了要寫碩士論文，才又再度回到出生地，從事文化田野調查工作。

本書初版時，官方只公告認定10個原住民族，當時撒奇萊雅族因大多住在阿美族落，而被視為阿美族。在2007年經官方公告承認撒奇萊雅族前後，他不遺餘力參與推動文化傳承。

對於認識台灣原住民族的文化、歷史充滿渴望，然而越深入了解，越覺得流失嚴重，尤其語言消失得更快，已經到了生死存亡的關鍵時刻。體認自身能力有限，僅能就專業所學做一些基礎記錄及調查工作，除了為自己族人的文化及歷史留下隻字片語，冀望更多有心人共同努力，將最能發揮台灣特色的原住民文化，延續在這一塊土地上。

繪圖者：

林順道 Nufu 努富

從小就很喜歡畫畫，經過自學摸索，目前從事電腦動畫與遊戲的專案美術指導，以及場景設計等相關工作。

經友人陳過介紹，有幸擔任本書畫者。當接過文稿時，才知道豐年祭也有神話傳說，而整本書新奇又有趣的故事，若非專程請教族中長者是聽不到的。原以為可以很容易的揣摩這些情節，但事實並非如此，因為長時間在台北工作很少回去，又為了畫出接近早期阿美族的感覺，雖然手邊有很多出版社及麗芬小姐提供的資料，但要將本身有限的記憶、現在時空，以及遠古流傳的故事，三者重新再結合，當中充滿挫折。尤其「巨人阿里嘎該」就重畫了三次以上！不免質疑自己畫圖能力，也可笑的懷疑自己是不是阿美族人？過程雖然煎熬，但無形中也感受到族人早期原始的美感。

◆ 卑南族

林志興 Agilasay 阿吉拉賽

他是族群融合的結果，也身體力行族群融合：他的爸爸是卑南族，媽媽是阿美族，他在21歲迷上一位排灣姑娘，和她廝守至今，生了兩位聰明可愛的女兒。

他生性樂觀、愛說話，從台下說到台上，從白天說到夢中；不過偶爾也會沉思，想到族人處境和前途時，就拿筆書寫或敲打鍵盤來宣洩情緒。

他生在阿美族部落，又隨爸媽住過達悟、排灣、布農等部落，大三那年才回到故鄉南王部落。考大學時無意間栽入人類學領域，從此死抱不放。21歲取得台大人類學學士、38歲取得碩士，後來又攻得博士學位，且仍一邊在國立台灣史前文化博物館工作，直到在副館長任內退休。

每每想到自己的工作、興趣和志業能吻合，他就嘿嘿地笑了起來，自覺幸福無人能及。

陳建年 Pau-dull 包杜魯

他是2000年金曲獎最佳男歌手獎和最佳作曲獎的雙料得主，之後更是入圍、獲獎不斷。從小就愛音樂，除了彈吉他之外，還會吹口琴、拉胡琴，也會自己作樂器（如排笛），但是，很少人知道他也很會畫畫。他不只琴棋書畫樣樣通，還是卑南勇士呢！精通柔道和跆拳道，曾在全國性比賽大顯過身手。

像他這樣才華洋溢的人，還真不多，如果要在演藝圈發展，可以大大的紅透半邊天。但是，他生性恬淡，只想當個盡責的人民保姆（已退休），與妻小共組溫馨家庭，閒暇時垂釣太平洋畔，夜來與二、三知音作伴，或彈或唱，愜意過人生。 他和他的外祖父陸森寶（著名卑南族民族音樂家）一樣，喜愛創作，只想把心中的感情唱出來，把好作品和大家分享，從來沒想到要出名獲利，卻自然實至名歸。

◆ 達悟族

故事採集者：

希南·巴娜妲燕 Sinan Panatayan

她回想過去小時候，在蘭嶼的生活方式很傳統，平時吃地瓜、芋頭、魚，聽父母親說故事，唱古調等等。但是，長大離開家鄉在台灣求學、工作之後，對族人的文化、歷史逐漸淡忘，唯一還熟悉的是自己的母語。

文明世界與傳統文化之間的衝突曾令她困惑：該擁抱現在，還是在乎自己族人的文化；經過多年的掙扎，已經整理出思緒，便是借重文字來記載屬於族人的故事、留住記憶中的一切。現在的蘭嶼雖然看不見濃濃的傳統味，但她深信達悟族無論在人文及生態方面都非常值得珍惜，並且讓她從傳統文化中找到了自信。她由衷感謝提供故事的長輩們、她的家人，以及張海嶼牧師和王榮基先生在母語拼音上的協助，更謝謝「三姊妹工作室」的姊姊們，給她充分的時間來完成這本書。

繪圖者：

席·傑勒吉藍 Si Cilcilan

他慶幸自己生長在蘭嶼，有湛藍的大海、蒼鬱的森林為伴。歡喜時他大聲吶喊與山海分享，悲傷時他獨自在山海裡療傷，美麗的蘭嶼給他生命、也給他力量。多年前，他目睹多位達悟族長老身穿戰服，遠到台北立法院前抗議請願，要求將核廢料遷出蘭嶼，令他十分動容且震撼。從此，他開始關心並參與社會運動，並回到蘭嶼學習傳統獵魚技術、做田野採集、古部落遺址調查、田野攝影等等。同時，以達悟傳統文化為創作題材，描繪出蘭嶼寧靜的美、動植物的鮮活，以及達悟族人的豐富表情，目前已舉辦過多次個展及聯展。

「飛魚」是朋友取的封號，而他也如同飛魚一樣充滿活力，曾數度帶領族人反核，以具體行動表現對大自然的尊重與蘭嶼的關懷。成立「黑翅膀工作室」專心投入藝術創作，「飛魚藝術咖啡屋」則是提供大家欣賞他創作的地方。2003年1月本書初版時，他剛好當爸爸，所以大家都改稱他為「飛魚夏曼」（「夏曼」是達悟男子婚後生子的稱法）。